# LADY LUCY'S SECRET; OR, THE GOLD THIMBLE

Lucy Ellen Guernsey

**NATAL PUBLISHING LLC**
*ARS LONGA, VITA BREVIS*

# CHAPTER I.

I WONDER whether, if you had seen Lady Lucy sitting at her work that warm August morning, you would have thought her a person to be envied. She certainly looked very pretty, and not at all unhappy, as she sat in her straight-backed chair, carrying her long-waisted, snugly-laced little figure very upright, her shoulders down, and her chin drawn in,—bridled, as the phrase went. In those days—for this was at the beginning of the eighteenth century—great attention was paid to the carriage of young ladies,—more than appears to be thought necessary at the present time, to judge by the attitudes into which I often see little girls throw themselves, even in company. They were taught to sit and stand very upright, to carry their arms carefully, to turn out their toes and hold up their heads. No stooping was permitted over books or work; and while Lady Lucy was living with her aunt Bernard, she used to have a bunch of knitting-needles stuck into her bodice, to keep her from "poking" over her work.

Lady Lucy was young,—only a little past eleven years old,—and small for her age: nevertheless, she was the rightful heir of the splendid room in which she now sat, with its heavy carved furniture, its worked tapestry hangings, and inlaid cabinets,—of the fine old house, Stanton Court,—of the lovely gardens and shrubbery which lay stretched before the windows, and the beautiful park, and many a farm and moorland besides. She could only just remember her mother as a delicate lady, with beautiful long black hair and dark eyes, who was very kind to her and used to talk to her in a musical, soft-sounding language, which was not English, nor at all like any tongue she ever heard nowadays. When Lady Lucy learned to be confidential with Cousin Debby, she told her of this strange language in which her mother used to talk; and Cousin Debby informed her that the language was Italian, and that some day she should learn it herself.

When Lucy thought of her mother, it was always as sitting down on the floor to play with her, or hearing her say her prayers, or else as she lay in her coffin all dressed in white, when Aunt Bernard would make the child kiss the cold face, and called her an unfeeling, heartless girl, because she had cried and screamed to get away and had declared that that was not her mother. Lucy almost thought that she began to hate Aunt Bernard from that moment. Certainly there was always war between them from that day; and, though Aunt Bernard was the stronger and compelled the child to obey, she never won her love.

It was not so very pleasant, after all, this being an heiress, with no father or mother to love and pet one, no little sisters for playmates to help dress the doll or nurse the kitten, or to make foxglove dolls and cowslip-balls, or tell tales in the seat under the tall old elm. Aunt Bernard said that, for her part, she meant to do her duty by the child: there would be people enough to spoil and flatter her by-and-by. I really think, too, that when she began she meant what she said,—though she was perhaps mistaken as to what constituted her duty but, as the time wore on, and she could not but see that Lucy disliked her, she began in her turn to dislike Lucy and the poor child led a hard life of it.

Aunt Bernard lived in a beautiful place. It was an old timbered house, of which the beams were black with age and the plastered spaces between marked off into patterns. There was a beautiful though not very large garden, with green alleys and grass-plots, where Lucy would have liked to play if she had been allowed, and where grew abundance of flowers. At the bottom of the garden was a tall hedge, clipped close and smooth like a wall, with arched openings leading through to another green, beyond which, again, was a pretty stream where ducks and geese, and one old swan, sailed up and down all day long.

Lucy would have enjoyed playing on the green, and sailing little boats upon the stream, and throwing bits of bread to the waterfowls but she was never allowed to do any of these things. If she ever ventured to run or romp, she was reminded that she was a lady,—a countess in her own right,—and that she must not demean herself like the parson's little girls, who worked in the hay-field, or gathered cowslips for wine in the meadows, or herbs and roots for their mother to distil into medicines and cordials. Lucy used many times to wish that she had been the daughter of that stout, good-natured gentleman and his plump, rosy little wife, who walked to church every Sunday morning followed by their ten children, two by two, and looking so happy and pleasant. True, the little Burgess girls hardly ever seemed to have new gowns or hoods, even for Sundays, and their weekday frocks were coarse and mended but she was sure that Polly and Dulcie Burgess were much happier than she was. But when she ventured to express this thought to Hannah, her aunt's waiting-woman, Hannah reproved her sharply, and added that it served Mrs. Kitty Lindsay right for marrying a poor parson, that she should have such a host of children and nothing to keep them decent.

Poor Lucy could not make hay, or gather primroses in the lanes, or carry jugs of skim-milk to the poor old people, as Polly Burgess did. She must practise on her lute so many hours a day, instead of singing sweet old country songs and ballads like Polly and her sister. She must work at her sampler and her satin stitches so many hours more, and read and write so much longer. She must read so many chapters in the Bible aloud to Aunt Bernard, taking them as they came, whether it were a long chapter of hard names and nothing else, or a beautiful story in the New Testament. She must learn her lesson standing in the stocks to make her turn her toes out, and carrying a heavy bag of beans upon her head that she might attain a good carriage, or strapped up to a back-board or lying flat upon the floor, to straighten her back.

If there was daylight enough after all this was done, she might walk up and down the green path in the garden and around the shrubbery for a certain length of time. There was one place in her walk where Lucy was out of sight of the garden-windows for some little distance and here she used to peep among the branches for the birds' nests, and strew for the robin-redbreasts the few crumbs she could contrive to save from her breakfast. There was a garden-seat, too, old and broken, where she could venture to rest a few minutes and look at the sky or the water, while she thought about her mother and wondered if she remembered her poor little girl who was so very, very unhappy and lonely without her.

Lucy did not think so much about her father. She had only seen him twice since she could remember, when he had come from the wars. She thought he must have been a good man, because her mother had been so happy when he came home; and she was sure he was kind to her and used to give her rides upon his shoulder or his foot. She remembered, too, the day when the news came of his death, and she had been dressed in black and told it was for her dear papa who had been killed in the wars abroad. But it was of her mother that she loved to think at such times, even though the remembrance made her feel more unhappy than ever.

Poor little Lucy! It was a sad, irksome life. It would have been dull enough if Aunt Bernard had been kind to her but she was not. She did not love the little girl. She envied her because Lucy was rich, and she herself poor, or, at least, not wealthy. She had hated her mother before her, and she visited it on her little daughter. Lucy could never do any thing right. Whether she sat or stood, ate or drank, worked, read, or played, Aunt Bernard always saw something to find fault with. Nor was fault-finding the worst. Aunt Bernard carried a fan with a long whalebone handle, and there were few days in which the impression of that whalebone was not printed upon Lucy's shoulders or arms, nor many weeks during which she was not sent supperless to bed in the dark.

She would have fared worse than she did, if Margery, the cook, had not pitied the child. Sometimes Margery would contrive to bring her a cake or a biscuit; and when Mrs. Bernard went away on a visit with her waiting-woman Hannah, Margery would make feasts for Lady Lucy in the kitchen, and sometimes allow her to bake little cakes for herself. These were Lucy's happy days, when she could sit in a corner of the great chimney and watch the cook bustling about her work, or the milkmaid bringing in her pails of fresh milk and carrying out buckets of whey to the pigs. It made no difference to Lucy that her aunt always forbade her going into the kitchen,—unless, indeed, it rather added to her pleasure to think that she was disobeying Aunt Bernard and for once having her own way. It was perhaps the worst result of that lady's system of management that Lucy learned to take pleasure in deceiving and outwitting her.

One day, however,—one memorable, miserable day,—all these surreptitious feasts came to a sudden end. I will tell you about it particularly, because it was the means of bringing about a great change in Lucy's manner of life.

On this day Aunt Bernard set out in her carriage to make a visit at Langham Hall, some twenty miles away. She was to stay over-night with Lady Langham and return home the next evening. She left Lucy plenty of work to do, and many injunctions as to her conduct, and threats as to what would happen if she were disobedient.

Lucy stood demurely at the door and watched the carriage out of sight and hearing. Then she started and ran like a hare down the garden, and through the gate in the holly hedge, to the water-side, but presently came running back to beg for some bits of bread to feed the swan.

"Bless the poor child!" said kind old Margery. "'Tis like a kitten let out of a basket, to be sure. But, Lady Lucy, my dear, had you not better do your tasks before you go to play?"

"I cannot do them all before my aunt comes home again,—no, not if I were to work all night, Margery!" said Lucy, shaking her head. "And if I have the least bit undone I shall be scolded and beaten as much as if I had not touched them: so where is the use? I may just as well play while I can."

"'Tis true what the child says," remarked Anne, the housemaid, as Margery looked grave: "my mistress has left her marking and open-hem enough for a grown woman, besides all her other tasks,—more shame to her, I say, to have no feeling for her own flesh and blood! Never mind,

Lady Lucy: I will take hold of it when my work is done, and you shall have one good play. But you must mind and wear your gloves and your hood, and not break your nails and scratch your hands with the brambles, or my mistress will find you out."

"I don't feel right about teaching and helping the child to deceive her aunt," said Margery, when Lucy had rather unwillingly gone to seek her hood.

"I don't care one pin," replied Anne, decidedly. "If my mistress treated any of us with any confidence, or put any trust in one, it would be different; but so long as she and Hannah are always spying and prying about, and won't believe a word one says, even though it should be gospel truth, why, they may just find out what they can, for all me. I shall just sit down and do up the child's open-hem for her, and my mistress may find out the difference if she can. It will not be the first trick I have played her in my time,—nor you either, Mistress Margery."

Margery sighed, and shook her head. She was not satisfied with Anne's reasoning, nor did her own conscience acquit her in the matter, but she was very fond of Lucy, and loved to see the child happy for once, as she said. So she set about making currant buns and a gooseberry fool—an old-fashioned country dish, than which there are few better—for Lucy's supper. But Lucy was not destined to the enjoyment of these dainties.

She played in the garden and down by the brook as long as she could see, forgetting for a while books, lute, and all the rest of her torments. She talked to Polly Burgess across the stream, and watched her as she milked her own little black Welsh cow, wishing all the time that she had a cow to milk and take care of. At last she yielded to Anne's entreaties that she would come in out of the dew and eat her supper.

She had just settled herself comfortably at the little table which Margery had set out in the corner, and was watching with quiet satisfaction the toasting of the currant buns, when the door of the kitchen was opened, and Aunt Bernard, entering quietly as usual, stood transfixed with amazement and anger at the sight which met her eyes. There was Lady Lucy, in the kitchen, actually leaning with both elbows on the table, and her chin resting on her hands, watching Margery, who was on her knees toasting the buns, and laughing and joking with old Roger, the cow-man; while Anne had actually a whole new mould candle lighted at her elbow, and was busily working at the open-hem ruffle!

Aunt Bernard had gone more than half her journey, when she was met by a messenger sent to tell her that the family at Langham Hall were in great trouble,—that the smallpox had broken out in the house, and my lady's two daughters were down with that dreadful disease, for which in those days no preventive was known. Of course all thought of the visit was now out of the question, and Aunt Bernard turned homeward in no good humour. It was destined to be a day of misfortunes; for about a mile from home the carriage broke down, and Aunt Bernard was obliged to walk home, in her best brocade and carriage-shoes, over a road far from good in the best of times, and now sloppy and dirty from two or three days' rain. It was in no placid mood, therefore, that she opened the kitchen-door, to find her family in her absence violating almost every rule she had ever laid down for them.

It was upon Lucy, as usual, that her wrath fell heaviest. The poor child had never in all her sad life been so berated. Ladies in those days were used to employ language for which in these a housemaid would be dismissed; and when Aunt Bernard was angry there were few names too hard to be bestowed upon Lucy. Nor was this the worst. Aunt Bernard declared that Lucy was the true child of her mother, that foreign woman who had deceived and ensnared her poor brother to his ruin; that her mother had been a liar, and worse; and that Lucy was fast following in her steps down to perdition.

As she went on, Lucy, who had seemed stunned at first, lifted up her head and looked Mrs. Bernard steadily in the face, while her colour rose, and her large black eyes flashed fire.

"Aunt Bernard, you are a wicked woman to speak so of my dear mother," said she. "Mamma was a lovely lady; and my father loved her. She is an angel now; and when you call her bad names, it is you that are the liar, and not she."

Aunt Bernard stood as if stunned, for a moment. Then she seized Lucy by the arm.

"Down on your knees, this moment!" said she, sternly, and at the same time trying to force her to kneel. "Down upon your knees, this moment, and beg my pardon!"

"I will not!" returned Lucy, resisting with all her strength. "I will never beg your pardon. I hate you, Aunt Bernard, with my whole heart! I would rather live with the dogs in the parson's kennel than with you."

Aunt Bernard said no more, but, dragging Lucy out of the kitchen, and up the stairs to a disused attic, she thrust her in by main force, and shut the door behind her. The maids could only guess what passed by hearing Lucy's cries and screams. Presently Aunt Bernard came down-stairs and into the kitchen, expecting to find Anne and Margery in a great fright She was mistaken.

"Mistress," said old Margery, rising, and standing before her with folded arms, "is it your purpose to let that child remain all night in that desolate chamber?"

"That is no business of yours, Margery; but, since you ask me, I will tell you that it is my purpose to keep her a prisoner, and upon prisoners' diet, and that of the sparest. She shall neither come out of that room, nor shall she see other food than brown bread and water, till she kneels to me and begs my pardon,—nor then, unless I see fit to grant it. I will break that proud spirit, or I will know why. Nay, I will not hear a word," she added, sternly, as she saw Margery preparing to speak. "You and Anne will find you have done the child little good with your coddlings and cossetings."

"Then, madam," said the old woman, not without dignity, "you will please suit yourself with another cook. I have served you for many a year, and did not think to leave you during my life; but I will never stay under a roof where an orphan child is so treated. The day after to-morrow is quarter-day: so you will please suit yourself with a cook."

"And with a housemaid also, mistress," said Anne. "'Tis well known that an orphan's curse will bring destruction upon the proudest house; and I, for one, have no wish to abide it. Every one knows how the lightning struck Farmer Dobson's stacks and barns after he turned his wife's poor daughter out of doors, and what happened to the uncle of the Babes in the Wood."

Anne spoke according to the superstitions of the time; nor was Mrs. Bernard's mind so free from it that a shudder did not pass over her at the girl's bold words. But she was proud and obstinate,—firm and dignified she called herself. Her own conscience told her that she was cruel and unforgiving,—that she visiting on Lucy's head not so much the child's fault as her own vexation. But she would not listen. Her evil passions were aroused, and had become her masters.

"You must do as you please," said she, coldly. "I shall doubtless find other servants in your place easier than you will find other services,— especially at your age, Margery."

"I can't help that," said Anne, tossing her head. "Better a crust in quietness than a full dish under the curse of the orphan."

Two or three days passed on, and nothing was seen of Lucy. She remained shut up in her attic chamber, visited by her aunt or Hannah once a day, with scanty and coarse provisions. Sometimes the girls, listening, heard her sobbing as if her heart would break, sometimes moaning faintly; but Mrs. Bernard kept close watch, and they could not get near her.

"I can't stand this any longer," said Anne to Margery, the third day. "The child will die before she will give way, and her blood will be on all our heads. I shall go to Parson Burgess and tell him the story. He is justice as well as parson; and we will see if something cannot be done." *

* In England, the rector, or minister, of a parish is not unfrequently a justice also.

"Do," said Margery. "No one can tell whether it will do any good; but things must not go on as they are. I know my mistress's temper but too well. It was just such a time as this with Lady Lucy which drove my poor young master to sea, where he perished miserably."

It was not long before Anne was at the parson's gate, where she found the children all assembled, some admiring and feeding with grass the two beautiful horses which stood before the door, some watching half timidly the negro servant who held them, and who was trying to coax the youngest little girl to come to him. Anne's tale was soon told to Polly, who, as the eldest, was exercising a sort of supervision over the little ones.

"What a shame!" exclaimed the warm-hearted girl, as Anne concluded her tale, which lost nothing from her manner of telling it. "Oh, if my father were only alone! There is a great gentleman with him, who came just now; and we must not interrupt him."

"Tell mother," said Dulcie, the second girl: "mother will know what to do. And here she comes now."

Mistress Burgess listened to Anne's repetition of the sad tale.

"Isn't it a shame, mother?" exclaimed the girls. "Poor little Lady Lucy!"

"Are you sure you are telling the truth, my girl?" asked Mistress Burgess, bending her mild, penetrating eyes on Anne's face, and hushing with an upraised finger the clamours of the children. "Recollect yourself; for this is a matter of the last importance, and you are come in the nick of time. The gentleman who arrived this morning is Lady Lucy's father."

"Why, mamma, I thought he was dead long ago!"

"And so thought every one; but it turns out a mistake. He was wounded and left for dead, and only recovered to find himself in a French prison, where he has languished all these years till just now that he has been exchanged; not by his own title,—for as Lord Stanton, he had been condemned to death, and had only saved his life by taking the name of his servant, who died in his cell. He has known naught of his own family,—not even that his poor wife was dead."

Anne was not a little daunted when she found herself in presence of the parson and his guest, the tall, stately soldier. But she was a girl of spirit, and confident in the goodness of her cause; and she told a simple, straight-forward story, from which all the cross-questioning of Dr. Burgess and Lord Stanton did not cause her to vary an inch.

"I thank you, my girl," said Lord Stanton, at last. "I shall not forget your services and, meantime, here is a token for you," (putting a gold piece in her hand). "You will please say nothing of this at the Grange till I come. I wish to see the state of things for myself, and will follow you directly."

"And a nice surprise it will be for my mistress," thought Anne, as she curtsied, and retired, well pleased with her day's work. "I am sure I will say nothing to spoil it."

"Do you think this girl's tale can be true?" asked Lord Stanton. "I know my sister Bernard for a hard, stern woman, who would have been my last choice for a guardian; but this seems beyond belief."

"Her cousin, Sir James Warden, doubtless acted for the best," said Dr. Burgess. "Mrs. Bernard has ever been counted an honourable woman, though somewhat stern and severe, especially with children. I have often pitied Lady Lucy, and would willingly have made her acquaintance, that she might amuse herself with companions of her own age; but her aunt has repelled all our advances. It may be that my good wife and myself have erred is the opposite direction, and allowed too much liberty to our young flock. I know that Mrs. Bernard is of that opinion,—which probably is one reason that she will not allow Lady Lucy to play with my girls, but I cannot think children spoiled who mind their mother with a word or look, and come to their parents with all their little secrets and confessions as freely as our young ones."

"Truly I should say not," returned Lord Stanton. "But I am impatient to see my poor little daughter. May I so far trespass upon your kindness as to ask Mrs. Burgess to take charge of her for a day or two till I can make arrangements for keeping her at home?"

"Surely, surely, my lord,—if she can live as we do. I will mention the matter to my wife."

Poor Lucy, on her hard bed, had fallen into an uneasy slumber, while her bread and water stood almost untouched upon the table. The three days of confinement and harsh treatment had made a great change in her appearance. She was thinner and paler, with dark purple marks under her eyes; and the scarlet traces of the blows she had received still showed plainly upon her thin white neck and arms. She had seen from the window her aunt go out for a walk, as usual, in the cool of the day, and had waited, watching and hoping that Anne or Margery would find a chance to speak to her through the key-hole, if no more. But no one came, and she had cried herself to sleep.

She was suddenly awakened by the sound of several voices upon the stairs. She distinguished Anne's, and then Hannah's, and then a stern, manly voice, which said,—

"If you do not open the door without delay, I will break it in. I will not be kept from my child."

Then the door was unlocked, and she saw Anne and Margery, Hannah, looking frightened and angry, and a tall, richly-dressed gentleman, whom she seemed directly to remember, and who caught her in his arms, calling her his darling, his poor, motherless, abused child.

"Are you really my father,—my own father who was dead?" she asked, at last, and leaning back to look at him.

"I am your own father, child, counted dead for so many years."

"And is mamma come alive again too?"

Lucy felt herself drawn into a closer embrace as her father whispered,—

"No, dear child: your precious mother cannot come again; but we shall go to her."

"And will you take me away and let me live with you?" asked Lucy. "Oh, papa, I will try to be so very good, if you will!"

"Yes, Lucy: you shall go with me this very night. Mistress Burgess will receive you."

"The child must not be removed till my mistress returns," said Hannah, tartly. "Her guardian put her in my mistress's care; and to him she is answerable,—not to a stranger."

Lord Stanton rose.

"She shall be removed without one moment's delay," said he, firmly. "I am her father. Let some one—you, my girl—" as he saw Anne—"bring something in which to wrap her. I will answer to my sister for what I do. Whether she can answer to me, is another matter."

Mrs. Bernard, returning from her walk, saw the servants and horses standing at Dr. Burgess's door; but she thought nothing of it, except to wonder what grand visitor had come to the parson's. Her meditations had not been very pleasant. She was beginning to get over her fit of anger, and to listen to two counsellors,—conscience and interest; and from neither of them did she obtain a great deal of comfort.

Conscience told her that she had given way to passion; that she had been harsh and cruel to a helpless child; that she had failed in her trust, and had roused, in the usually timid and yielding girl, pride and obstinacy equal to her own.

Interest told her that she had made an enemy of Lucy; that she had failed to win the child's affection or confidence; that she had no hold upon her but sheer physical force. Sir James Warden, Lucy's cousin and guardian, might see fit to remove her at any time; and no doubt Lucy would look upon change as for the better. The child herself would be no great loss; but with her would go the three hundred pounds a year allowed for her guardianship, and with that the carriage, the extra servants, perhaps the very house in which she lived and which belonged to the Stanton-Corbet estate.

She had no claim upon the property save what grew out of her care of Lucy. She was the daughter of Lord Stanton's step-mother, and had been brought up with him: that was all the relationship. It would have been the part of wisdom, interest told her, to have acquired such a hold upon the little girl's regards as would have given her a lifelong influence over the young heiress. Instead of that, she had allowed her hatred of her step-brother's foreign wife to cause her to tyrannize over his daughter.

Lucy had never loved her, and she had long since lost even the slight hold upon her respect which she had once possessed. It was probably too late to mend matters now, even if her pride would have allowed her to stoop to a child; but Mrs. Bernard resolved that Lucy should be forgiven and released as if she had actually begged pardon, and that henceforth she would allow her more liberty.

In this frame of mind she came home, to be met by the news that Lucy's father had returned and carried her away, leaving a note to explain his proceedings. What this note contained no one ever knew.

Mrs. Bernard read it and crushed it up in her hand without any remark. Then she bade Hannah pack Lady Lucy's clothes and other possessions and send them to the parsonage. She had all but idolized her step-brother, and had shed many tears for his loss; but she took no steps to see him, nor did she ever again mention his name. She continued for many years living in the same house, seeing no company, never going out even to church, and refusing to speak to any member of Dr. Burgess's family if by any chance she met them.

She had indulged pride and self-will till they had become absorbing passions over which she exerted no control. Some time after, Lady Lucy made more than one effort to see and conciliate her aunt; but Mrs. Bernard sternly repelled all her advances, and lived and died alone.

Meantime, Lady Lucy was most warmly received at the parsonage, installed in the best room, and treated with all the care and kindness which Mrs. Burgess and her daughters had to bestow, till her father came to carry her home to Stanton Court, where he had engaged an elderly lady—a cousin of his mother—to take care of her. Lord Stanton stayed a few days with Lucy, and then went abroad once more, leaving his daughter to the care of Cousin Deborah Corbet.

# CHAPTER II.

LUCY had been about five weeks under the charge of Cousin Deborah at the time our story begins,—weeks so quiet and happy, so free from care and fault-finding, that the little girl sometimes wondered whether she were living in the same world. Nothing seemed the same about her but Anne, who had come from the Grange to live at Stanton Court and attend upon Lady Lucy.

Cousin Deborah, for her part, would have preferred to do without Anne. She foresaw that Lucy would have formed undesirable and wrong habits under such a rule as that of Aunt Bernard, and she thought it would be more easy to break up these habits if the little girl had no one about her but such persons as she knew and could trust. But Anne's services had been too important to go unrewarded: she had lost her place from her devotion to Lady Lucy's interests, and she was devotedly attached to the child: so Cousin Deborah resolved to make the best of it.

It may easily be guessed that Anne was not at all unwilling to accompany Lady Lucy, or to exchange the close housekeeping of the Grange for the liberality of Stanton Court. Margery might have come, too, and both Lady Lucy and Anne begged her to do so; but Margery refused.

"I am not going to leave my old mistress, now that she is in trouble and disgrace," said she. "I shall stay and stand by her. She will find it hard to suit herself, with all these stories flying about the country. She is growing infirm in body and, I believe, in mind; and I will not leave her with no one about her whom she can trust but Hannah."

The stories to which Margery referred were exaggerated and distorted accounts of her mistress's treatment of Lady Lucy. The maids at the parsonage had gossiped, of course, as well as the milkmaid at the Grange. Every one in the village knew that Lady Lucy's father had found his daughter locked in an upper room alone, with nothing to eat but a crust of brown bread,—some said, not even that,—and had taken her away without seeing his sister or waiting for his child's clothes to be packed up. This was a fine nucleus for the story, which grew, like a snowball, every time it was turned over, till many people actually believed that Mrs. Bernard had gone deliberately to work to kill her niece by cruelty, that she might have the use of her property.

"I am sure it is no more than she deserves," said Anne, tossing her head.

"Perhaps so; but, Anne, if we come to talk of deserts, where should any of us be?"

"She has got Hannah," said Anne.

"Yes; and that is another reason for my staying. I don't trust Hannah. No, Anne: I love Lady Lucy, but I shall not leave Mrs. Bernard. Her husband was kind to mine when he needed kindness; her son was my foster-child, and dear to me as my own; and, for their sakes as well as hers, I shall stay."

And so Margery stayed; and, when Hannah left, she became in time the sole servant in the lonely, deserted Grange House, where Mrs. Bernard wore her life away in bitter recollections, with nothing to sustain her but her own pride and resentment.

Lucy had learned no lessons, nor performed any tasks, as she was accustomed to call them, since she came to Stanton Court. She had suffered greatly in health under Aunt Bernard's discipline, and especially under the last shock. She was timid, nervous, and depressed, afraid to speak, afraid to make a natural motion in presence of her elders, unable to imagine that any one could be kind to her or love her except Anne. She slept badly, and awoke feverish and without appetite; she was very soon tired with any exertion; and she had all the time a little, hard cough.

Cousin Debby was used to children. She had brought up six girls of her own, all of whom she had nursed through a somewhat delicate and sickly childhood, to be women of at least average health and strength. She saw that of lessons Lucy had lately had more than enough; and she wisely concluded that Lucy's health and spirits were to be cultivated, even at the expense of her present improvement in knowledge.

"A great many women get through the world pretty well without knowing much either of books or music," said she to her cousin, Lord Stanton; "but weak backs and nerves, and fits of vapours and hysterics, unfit a woman for any usefulness whatever. The child has been overworked, and needs rest."

And Lord Stanton had agreed with Cousin Deborah, and had bid her take her own course with Lucy. So, for the first few weeks, Lucy did little but run about the garden and grounds, and take rides on the donkey, with Cousin Debby walking by her side. But this morning Cousin Debby had decided she should begin some lessons again. So Lucy had learned a spelling-lesson, and practised on her lute for half an hour, and was now to do her task of sewing.

"What sort of work have you done most of?" asked Cousin Debby.

"Embroidery, and open-hem, and marking, and fine darning," said Lucy; "and oh, Cousin Debby, how I hate them all!"

Lucy looked scared as soon as she had said the words. Such a speech made in Aunt Bernard's hearing would have insured her an hour's additional work, if not a slap from the fan handle across her fingers; but Cousin Debby only smiled. She was glad to see that Lucy was beginning to feel a little freedom with her.

"Suppose, then, we try something else," said she. "The poor woman who lives at the porter's lodge has a pair of twins, born this morning; and she is but poorly provided with clothes for them. Suppose I cut out a flannel petticoat for one of them and show you how to make it?"

"I shall like that," said Lucy. "Dolly Burgess used to do things for poor people, I know. And please, cousin, do you think I might carry it to her myself? I should so like to see a little baby near by."

"You shall carry it to the baby yourself certainly," said Cousin Debby, smiling; "and you shall go with me this afternoon, when your sewing is done, to take the poor woman some broth which cook is making for her. So now be industrious, and see how much you will accomplish while I am gone. Have you a work-box of your own?"

"No, cousin: I kept my working-things in a corner of Aunt Bernard's table-drawer."

Cousin Debby took a bunch of keys from the little basket of keys which hung at her side, and, opening a tall cabinet which stood at one side of the fireplace, she took out a beautiful box. The sides were formed of ivory, inlaid with many curious figures in a black wood, which Cousin Debby told Lucy was ebony. She set the box on the little table in the bow-window where Lucy was sitting, and unlocked it by the little gold key which hung to the handle.

Lucy uttered an exclamation of delight. There were scissors and knives of various kinds, with gold and enamelled handles; there were bobbins, tooth-picks, and stilettos, and more other implements than you can mention, all ornamented in the same way, and a beautiful little crystal bottle of attar of roses, which still retained its perfume.

"This was your dear mother's work-box," said Cousin Debby; "and some day it shall be yours."

"When?" asked Lucy.

"When I see whether you are careful enough to be trusted with such valuable things," answered Cousin Debby. "You may keep it here upon the table, if you please, and lay your own thimble and scissors in this vacant place. I suppose your mother's thimble will be too large for you. Try it on."

Lucy slipped her finger into it.

"It is too large but I can wear it," said she. "Please let me use it this morning, Cousin Debby."

"No, not this morning. You might lose it; and, besides, there is a hole in it, which needs mending. I will send it to Exeter, when I can, and have it repaired and made a little smaller. Now go at your work; and if you have finished it by the time I come down, we will go to the lodge and see the little twins."

"What are you going to do, Cousin Debby?"

"I am going into the green chamber, to look over some drawers."

Left to herself, Lucy worked very industriously for half an hour. She kept the work-box open before her, and now and then she glanced at the contents. But Lucy was not used to working without being over-looked; and she had never been trusted in all her life.

Presently she dropped her work in her lap, and began to take out the articles in the work-box one by one and lay them upon the table.

At last she put on the thimble and began sewing with it. She took a few stitches with great satisfaction,—when all at once the eye of the needle found out the hole in the top of the thimble, and entered pretty deeply under Lucy's finger-nail. Now, there are few things more provocative of hasty action than a prick under the nails. Lucy dropped her work and gave her hand a sudden shake,—when off flew the thimble through the long window which opened to the terrace.

At the same moment she heard Cousin Debby coming down-stairs, stopping on the landing to talk with the housemaid. Hastily restoring the other articles to their places, Lucy peeped out to see what had become of the thimble. There it lay, just under one of the low flower-vases which adorned the terrace, half hidden under a broad-leaved plant which grew there. Lucy could see it plainly, and was just going to step out of the window to recover it, when Cousin Debby came out at the hall door and along towards the bow-window.

Hastily Lucy shrank back, and resumed her work, her fingers trembling and her heart sick with fear. Cousin Debby would no doubt see the thimble, and then all would be over.

"Well, Lucy, how has the work progressed?" asked Cousin Debby, pausing before the open window.

"Not very well," said Lucy, trying to speak quietly. "I pricked my finger, and I had to stop and wait for it to be done bleeding."

"Let me see," said Cousin Debby. "Why, that is a deep prick! You had better not sew any more just now, lest it should inflame and be troublesome. Run and get your hood, and we will walk down to the lodge."

Lucy's heart sank deeper still; but she dared not disobey. The best way would have been to tell the plain truth and pick up the thimble openly; but this she dared not do. She had been so severely treated for the least fault, that she had learned the habit of concealing every thing. She went up-stairs and put on her hood, expecting all the time to hear her name sharply called and feel her poor little fingers and arms tingle and burn from the application of a whalebone or ratan. Nothing of the sort happened, however.

When she came down, Cousin Debby was standing talking with the old gardener about some plants.

"You will be sure and remember, Robbins?" said she.

"Yes, madam,—oh, yes: I never forgets any thing," said Robbins.

"I dare say he will never think of it again," said Cousin Debby, as they walked away. "The poor old man grows more and more forgetful every day."

Lucy had a pleasant walk, and enjoyed very much seeing the dear little babies and holding one of them in her arms. The good woman lamented her want of baby-clothes; and Cousin Debby promised to see what she could find for them.

"You did not tell her that I was making a petticoat for the baby," Lucy ventured to observe, as they left the lodge to return home.

"No," replied Cousin Debby: "I thought it better to wait till the petticoat was finished. Something might happen to prevent your sewing, or you might be wanting in perseverance and then the poor woman would be disappointed. Do you know the meaning of 'perseverance'?"

"No, ma'am."

"Why do you not ask, then?"

"Aunt Bernard would never let me ask questions," replied Lucy. "She said it was not proper."

"There are times when it is not proper for little girls to ask questions," said Cousin Debby,—"as, for instance, in company, or when they interrupt their elders by so doing. But, Lucy, I want you always to feel free to ask me any questions you please when we are alone together. I may not always see fit to answer you; but I shall never be displeased at your asking, so that you do it in a proper spirit."

"What do you mean by a proper spirit?" Lucy ventured to inquire.

"Perhaps I can illustrate the matter best by telling you what is not a proper spirit. If I should tell you it was time to go to bed, and you should ask, in a fretful tone, 'Why must I go to bed now? Why cannot I sit up as long as you do?' That would be an improper spirit. But if you should obey directly, and should then ask, 'Why must little girls go to bed earlier than grown-up people?' because you wished to know the reason, I should then be ready to tell you all I know about the matter.

"Sometimes children ask impertinent questions,—as if you were to see me reading a letter and should ask whom it was from. Sometimes, too, they ask silly and troublesome questions, just to hear themselves talk,—which is a very disagreeable habit.

"Your asking the meaning of the word 'perseverance' would be a proper question; and I am very glad to answer it. To persevere in any thing you undertake to do is to keep at it till it is finished. If you work steadily at the baby's petticoat at all proper times till it is done, you will persevere. Now do you understand?"

"Yes, ma'am," replied Lucy. "I think it is pleasant to understand."

All this time the thought of the thimble was in Lucy's mind, lying under all her other thoughts, as a stone lies under a running stream. It did not make her so unhappy as it ought to have done; for, unluckily, Lucy was used to having such concealments and to hiding her faults as long as possible. She was not miserable at the thought that she had disobeyed and deceived her cousin: she only thought how she would be punished if the thimble were lost.

Aunt Bernard had never taught her to exercise her conscience—to do things because they were right, or refrain from them because they were wrong. But she felt in a great hurry to get back to the Hall, in order that she might find the thimble and restore it to its place before it was missed.

She was, therefore, not very well pleased when Cousin Debby said that, as the day was cool, they would walk to the village and call upon the rector's family, adding, "You will be glad to see Polly and Dulcie again; and, as little Willy Mattison is here, we will send him to bring down the donkey, that you may ride back."

Lucy would much rather have gone home; but she dared not object. She could not see any way to help herself: so she put the thought of the thimble as far away as she could, and resolved to make the best of matters.

The village church and parsonage lay about a mile from Stanton Court, and the walk to it was a lovely one,—through the woods, and along the banks of that very stream by which Lucy had stolen away to feed the swans. Now and then they passed a tiny waterfall; and more than once a lovely little spring came dripping down the rock, and collected in a little basin before it ran into the brook. On a stone by one of these springs sat a square wooden cup, roughly hewn out of a piece of hard wood; and here they stopped to drink. Cousin Debby knew the names of many of the plants, and the ways and habits of the birds and insects, and she told Lucy many interesting tales of their doings and customs. It would have been a very delightful walk if it had not been for that unlucky thimble and, even as it was, Lucy enjoyed it greatly, as well as the visit which followed.

Polly and Dulcie were strong, healthy, high-spirited girls, and, with their warm hearts and truthful ways, were as good companions as could be found for the poor, crushed, reserved little lady. So Cousin Debby thought; and she resolved to encourage a friendship between them. They gave Lucy a warm welcome, and did their best to entertain her,—showing her their gardens, the grotto which they were ornamenting with shell-work after the fashion of the time, and finally took her into the meadow, to show her Polly's little hornless cow, which was as tame and almost as playful as a kitten. Lucy looked across the stream into her aunt's garden, and up at the house where she had spent so many dreary hours, with a feeling of wonder.

"There is Mrs. Bernard now, walking on the green," said Polly. "Poor lady, how lonely she must be! I can't help feeling sorry for her, after all."

"I don't feel sorry for her," said Lucy, under her breath. "I hate her; and I should like to see her served just as she served me."

Lucy said these words with all energy which showed that she was thoroughly in earnest, and which made the gentle little Dulcie look up with surprise and horror.

"Oh, Lady Lucy, you should not feel so! It is not right. If she has treated you ever so bad, you ought to forgive her."

"Aunt Bernard never forgave me or anybody," returned Lucy. "She said once that she never forgave or forgot; and I have heard Margery say that she would never answer her own son's letter, when he wrote begging her pardon for running away to sea."

"Then she is a wicked woman, and you should not try to be like her," said plain-spoken Polly.

"Aunt Bernard said God hated sinners," persisted Lucy. "She said he hated me."

"I don't believe that," said Polly. "I mean to ask my father. Anyway, Lady Lucy, it was not much like hating you when God brought back your father from the prison and gave you such a nice home and such a nice lady to take care of you."

Lucy looked puzzled. "Did he do that? I never thought of that."

"Of course he did. He gives us all things. That is the reason we call him our Father, I suppose."

"I never thought of that," said Lucy, again. "I thought he was like a great king, who sat up in heaven and did not care what happened, only to punish people when they do wrong. I never thought of his being any thing like my father."

"You ought to think so; and you ought to love him, too," said Polly. "The catechism says our duty towards God is to love him with all our might; and it is in the Bible, too. And I am sure you ought to forgive Mrs. Bernard."

"I can't," returned Lucy. "You don't know how she treated me, Polly."

"I know she was shamefully cruel to you; but, Lady Lucy," added Polly, reverently, "you know she could not treat you so ill as our Lord was treated; and he forgave all his enemies, even on the cross. And, besides, you know God will not forgive you unless you forgive your aunt."

"It don't seem as if I could," said Lucy; and she looked again at the stately figure of Aunt Bernard, as she passed and repassed the archway in the holly hedges. "Oh, she was so hard,—so hard upon me!" she repeated, bitterly. "She never let me be happy one minute, if she could help it. And she abused my mamma. She called her a liar and an outlandish witch. No, Polly: I can't. I do hate her, and I always shall."

"But, Lady Lucy, what will become of you when you die, if you go on so?" argued Dulcie. "You know you cannot go to heaven unless you do forgive your enemies and are in charity with all men; and you know your mamma is in heaven," she added, in a low voice.

"And you cannot go to heaven unless God forgives you, either," added Polly. "You know we all do a great many wrong things, that need to be forgiven."

Lucy thought of the thimble lying under the aloe-leaf on the terrace. "Don't talk about it any more," said she, abruptly. "See, there is your mother calling us. I dare say Cousin Debby is ready to go home."

But Cousin Debby was not quite ready. Mrs. Burgess, in her hospitable kindness, would by no means allow them to depart without refreshment. The table was most invitingly set out in the great, cool parlour,—the parsonage had no other rooms below than the parlour and kitchen, and a room behind, which served the doctor for a study,—and Cousin Deborah and Lady Lucy must eat curds and cream and apricots and seed-cake and drink each a glass of gooseberry wine.

While they were chatting around the table, a shower came up, and Cousin Deborah concluded to wait until it was over. The weather partly cleared up towards evening, and they set out for home. But, before they reached Stanton Court, the rain poured down again, and they arrived at home wet to the skin.

Anne hurried Lucy off to bed, dosing her with warm gruel, lest she should take cold: so, of course, all chance of searching for the thimble was out of the question.

The next morning, before her cousin was dressed, Lucy ran down-stairs and out upon the terrace. Breathlessly she hurried to the flower-pots opposite the bow-window, and lifted the broad leaves one after the other.

The thimble was not there.

She stood bewildered for a moment, when it suddenly flashed across her mind that some one might have found it and put it away.

She hurried to the parlour. No: it was not in the box. It was lost!

# CHAPTER III.

"WHAT are you doing with the box, Lucy, my dear?" asked Cousin Debby, opening the door.

"I—I was looking to see whether I put my thimble away." Lucy had given a guilty start, and stammered so, as she spoke, that any other child would have been at once suspected of lying.

But she was always so timid and frightened that Cousin Debby did not think of any thing being the matter, except that Lucy had been in doubt about her thimble.

"Did you think you had lost it, then?" she asked.

"I could not be sure. I did not remember," said Lucy, stammering more and more. "Please, Cousin Deborah, do not be angry with me."

"You poor little dear, how scared you are! You are all in a tremble, and your little face is as white as your kerchief," said Cousin Deborah, sitting down, and taking Lucy on her knee. "Lucy, my child, I do not wish you ever to be afraid of me, even if you have done wrong. Try to have confidence in me and think that I am your friend."

Lucy did not answer.

And Cousin Deborah, seeing that she still trembled, thought best to divert her from her fright.

"See here, my love, your stay-lacing is not fastened, nor your shoes properly buckled. Your cap and kerchief, too, are soiled, and need changing; nor do I think these little finger-ends have seen the water this morning. Did Anne dress you?"

"No, Cousin Debby: I dressed myself. I did not think it was any harm," said poor Lucy, who was so used to being blamed, whatever she did, that she was by no means sure she had not committed a grave offense in being her own dressing-maid.

"There is no harm in that, my child. I am glad to have you learn to do every thing for yourself; but you must be neat and careful about it, and try always to look like a lady. I suppose, however, you were in a great hurry to find your thimble: so I will excuse you this time. Now go back to your room and make yourself neat, and then we will have prayers."

As Lucy went back to her room, she was conscious of a new feeling in regard to what she had done. She had often before been terrified at the consequences of wrong-doing; but of the action itself she had thought very little. But now, as she thought of having disobeyed and deceived kind

Cousin Deborah, she felt sorry for and ashamed of her sin, as well as alarmed for the punishment she expected to receive whenever the thimble should be missed. And she felt that she should continue to be sorry, even if she were never punished at all.

"Oh, if I could only find it," she thought, "I would never, never be so naughty again."

She made herself as neat as she could, and was just finishing her dressing operations, when Anne entered.

"So, my lady, you are grown an early riser, and very independent, to be sure," said she, not very well pleased. "How long since you were so grand?"

"Why, Anne, you know I always dressed myself at Aunt Bernard's. And Cousin Debby says it is a very good thing. But I was in such a hurry this morning that I forgot to wash my hands or buckle my shoes; and Cousin Debby sent me back. Please get me a clean cap, Anne."

"Ay, you need one. See how you have tumbled your ruffles by throwing your cap down anyhow, instead of setting it tidily on the top of a chair-post, or some such place. What would Mrs. Bernard say to that, think you?"

"She would box my ears, I suppose," said Lucy: "so I am very glad she is not here. Don't be cross, please, Anne. I do like you to dress me; but, you know, I must do as Cousin Debby says."

"Of course you must," replied Anne, in a mollified tone,—"and all the more that she is so good to you. But I can tell you, Lady Lucy, she can be cruel strict, too. You ought to hear how she talked to Jenny housemaid because she told her a fib about the linen. She made her cry, I promise you; and she said she could put up with any thing better than a lie: so you must be careful, Lady Lucy. But, goodness gracious me, child! What is the matter, that you turn so pale?"

"Oh, Anne, I have done such a dreadful thing!" said poor Lucy. "And I have told Cousin Debby a lie, too! Oh, what shall I do?"

"Tell me all about it," said Anne. "I will put a clean tucker in your bodice, meantime."

Lucy related the story, with many injunctions not to tell.

Anne listened attentively, and shook her head when it was finished.

"'Tis a bad business," said she. "I am much afraid you will never see the thimble again. There was a tramper woman here yesterday, with her child on her back; and she went along the whole length of the terrace,— the impudent beggar! Nothing less would serve her; and I doubt she has seen the thimble and picked it up. You see, if old Robbins had found it, he would have brought it back: he would as soon cut his head off as steal, would Robbins. But it won't do to ask him about it; because that would let out the secret."

"Then, what shall I do?" asked Lucy, in a despairing tone. "As soon as ever I come to do my task of sewing, the thimble will be missed."

"Hark! There is Mrs. Corbet calling you," said Anne. "Go down now,—there's a dear,—and I will think the matter over and see what can be done."

"You have been a long time," said Cousin Deborah. "What hindered you?"

"Anne had to sew a new tucker in my bodice," said Lucy.

"Anne must learn to have your things ready beforehand. But never mind, now. Come and read the psalm."

It was rather hard for Lucy to bring her mind to the task, but she did really wish to please Cousin Deborah: so she took pains, and succeeded tolerably well.

Cousin Deborah went back and repeated one of the last verses:—

"'If I regard wickedness in my heart, the Lord will not hear me,'" said she.

"Do you know what that means, Lucy?"

Lucy had never been much accustomed to think about what she read, and she had no answer ready.

"Let us see if we cannot find a meaning in it," said Cousin Deborah. "How can any one regard wickedness in his heart?"

"By wanting to do what is wrong, I suppose," replied Lucy, after some thought.

"Yes,—by wishing and intending to do what is wrong. If you were to pray to God for his blessing, while all the time you were wishing and meaning to do something wicked, God would not regard your prayer. You would not have any right to expect it. It would be no reason for his not hearing you, that you had already done even a very wicked thing, if you were truly sorry for your wickedness and asked your Father in heaven to forgive you for his dear Son's sake. But if you meant to do the same thing right over again as soon as you had a chance, you could not expect him to hear you. You know he sees all your thoughts and feelings, whether you speak them out or not. I can only guess, at the best, what you are thinking about; but the Lord knows the very thoughts of all our hearts."

These words, as you may suppose were any thing but comfortable to poor Lucy. She had heard enough of God before,—and more than enough;

for Aunt Bernard used to frighten her, many a time, by telling her that he was angry with her and would destroy her. But Cousin Debby spoke in a very different way,—as if she feared him and loved him too. Polly Burgess, too, spoke of loving him, and said he was like her own father, only a great deal better and kinder. He had delivered her dear papa from the French prison and brought him safely home to her, and had given her dear, good Cousin Debby to take care of her,—so Polly said. And she prayed with Cousin Debby every morning and night that God would take care of papa in the war and bring him safe home again.

But, if what Cousin Debby said was true, what was the use of her praying? She had told several lies about the thimble; and she knew she meant to tell another and a worse one. She had planned to tell Cousin Debby that the window was left open and the box unlocked, and that the beggar-woman must have come in and stolen the thimble.

"But I will not say a word about it, unless she asks me; and, anyway, I dare say she did take the thimble from the terrace: so that will be partly true. And I will be just as good as I can be about every thing else, and I will never tell a lie again after this time."

So Lucy resolved; but, somehow, the resolution did not seem to afford her much comfort. She did her lessons unusually well, and received great commendation; but Cousin Debby's praises did not give her the same pleasure that they had done yesterday. Her mind was beginning to open to the sense of right and wrong, and she felt that she did not deserve them.

Then came the sewing; and Lucy's heart sank as Cousin Debby opened the work-box.

Strangely enough, however, she did not appear to miss the thimble, although the little satin-lined compartment where it belonged was plainly empty.

"Now let me see how diligent you can be," said she, as she unfolded the little petticoat. "You have done this very neatly, Lucy,—as well as I could have done it myself. Aunt Bernard must have taken great pains with your needlework. There are very few girls of your age who can work so neatly. You see you have at least one thing for which to thank her."

Lucy did not feel so very grateful at that moment; but she agreed to all Cousin Debby said, and took up her work, resolved to do her very best. She hoped Cousin Debby would go away and leave her to herself, as she did yesterday.

But, instead of doing so, she sat down in the bow-window and occupied herself in darning some beautiful old lace. She told Lucy this lace had belonged to her grandmother and should some day be hers; and she related many interesting anecdotes of this same grandmother, and of other ladies, members of the Stanton and Corbet families, whose portraits hung in the long picture-gallery up-stairs.

In spite of her trouble of mind, Lucy could not help being interested in these tales. And she was surprised, when the clock struck eleven, to find that she had come to the end of her work.

"See, Cousin Deborah: is not this finished?" she asked, as she held it up for inspection.

"It is finished, and very nicely, too," replied Cousin Deborah, taking the little garment out of her hand and looking it over. "I have found several other articles which will be useful to the poor woman. And after dinner, if it is fine, you shall go with Anne and carry them to her; afterwards you may ride as far as the village shop and buy me some needles and tape. Now go and play a little; and, when you hear the clock strike the half-hour, come in and get ready for dinner."

"Where are you going, Cousin Deborah?" Lucy ventured to ask, as she saw her cousin putting up her own work.

"I am going to my room for a while. Now run away and play."

Lucy was glad to hear that her cousin was going to her room. It was upon the other side of the house, and quite away from the terrace. And Lucy resolved that she would improve the opportunity and spend the half-hour in one more hunt for the thimble.

But in vain did she search under the leaves of the broad-leaved aloe, scratching her hands sadly with the sharp thorns. Her thimble was clearly not there.


"How did you scratch your hands so, my dear?" asked Cousin Deborah, when Lucy came down to dinner.

"I was looking at a bird's nest in the holly-bush, Cousin Debby," replied Lucy, in a low voice.

"You are quite sure you have not been at the gooseberry-bushes, Lucy?"

"Yes, ma'am. I have not been near them." Lucy was telling the truth this time, and spoke in tolerably steady tones but her conscience reproached her at the very moment, for she knew she had told another lie, in spite of all her resolutions. The rapid multiplication of lies has long been proverbial.

People in those days dined early: so that twelve was a fashionable hour. It was not quite noon when Cousin Debby and Lucy sat down to dinner.

Lucy had all her life been limited and scrimped as to her food. Aunt Bernard's housekeeping was far from liberal, at the best. True, she had always some sort of meat for dinner; but of this Lucy seldom got more than a very small taste, and right glad was she to be helped to enough of the batter-pudding, or dumpling cooked with the meat, to stay her hunger. Of tart, pudding, or any thing of that sort, she never tasted save by stealth when Margery or Anne would smuggle away a bit for her.

But Cousin Debby had very different notions. She helped Lucy liberally to the excellent roast-beef, and afterwards gave her a whole custard. Nor did she season these dainties with constant reproofs, or count every mouthful and accuse the child of gluttony because she had a good appetite. On the contrary, she smiled to see Lucy's plate emptied the second time, and said she was glad to see her enjoy her dinner.

"Think, Lucy, who it is that has given you all these good things," said Cousin Deborah, "and then your returning thanks will not be mere empty, formal words."

As Lucy stood up and repeated her "grace after meat," a good old custom which seems to have gone quite out of fashion, she thought, "He gave me this nice dinner, too. I do wish I could be good, when he is so good to me!"

Often had Lucy been required to say those words when the whole dinner-hour had been one of misery to her,—when she had nothing, as it seemed to her, to be thankful for but sharp words, hard crusts, and harder raps from Aunt Bernard's knife or fan handle,—when her heart was bursting with a sense of oppression and unkindness. Then she had never thought of their meaning, but only how to say them so that she should not earn another red ridge upon her neck or arms.

Now she thought of their sense, and really felt thankful to God for the nice meal and the love which seasoned it. But still that verse recurred to her mind:

"'If I regard wickedness in my heart, the Lord will not hear me.'"

"Now you may read to me a while; and after that, you and Anne can set out upon your expedition. I believe I will not go out to-day."

"Don't you feel well, Cousin Deborah?" asked Lucy.

"Yes, my dear; but I am somewhat tired. I am an old woman, you know, and cannot run about all day without being fatigued, as you young folks do."

"Are you really old, Cousin Debby?" asked Lucy, timidly.

"Yes, my dear: I am past sixty years old. I can just remember the day when King Charles the First was put to death; and I shall never forget the day that his son, Charles the Second, entered London after his restoration. I saw the long procession, and all the shows, and the feasts and bonfires in the streets. And I well remember the dreadful days of the great plague: though we did not live in London then, but some miles distant."

"Please, Cousin Deborah, I wish you would tell me some stories about those times," Lucy ventured to say. "It is so much nicer than reading them out of the history books."

"Well," said Cousin Deborah, smiling, "you certainly pay me a high compliment."

"It was not a compliment," said Lucy. "It was true."

"Compliments may be true as well as false, Lucy. But I will make a bargain with you. I will tell you stories for half an hour after dinner, provided you will work at the same time."

"Well," said Lucy, with great satisfaction. "What shall I do?"

"Suppose you begin to knit a pair of nice warm woollen stockings for poor Dame Higgins at the almshouse, whose hands are crippled by the rheumatism. You can easily have them ready against winter. I have plenty of good strong worsted."

"I shall like that," said Lucy. "It is so much nicer to think that I am working for people than just to work, work, stitch, stitch, without ever knowing what one is working for."

"I agree with you, Lucy. But you must be faithful in fulfilling your part of the bargain, or I shall consider myself released from mine."

The stocking was soon set up, and Lucy worked for an hour without once looking at the clock to see what time it was, while Cousin Deborah told her tales of the great civil war, which she had heard from her father and mother.

"Now you may go and get ready for your ride," said Cousin Deborah. "You will find the bundle of baby-linen upon my table, and cook Will give you some biscuit to carry to the poor woman. After you have been at the lodge, you may ride down to the shop and buy me a paper of needles, and two sticks of bobbin like the bit which is tied round the bundle. Take that for a sample; and here is sixpence, which you may spend for yourself, if you please. I dare say you and Anne will be glad of a cake apiece at the end of your journey."

"How good you are, Cousin Debby!" exclaimed Lucy. "You just seem to let me do things because I like them. I do love you dearly!"

And Lucy threw her arms round her cousin's neck and kissed her heartily. She had never yet kissed Aunt Bernard of her own accord. "Oh, how I do wish I could be a good girl!"

"Why, I think you are a tolerably good girl, as little girls go," said Cousin Deborah, returning the kiss, "though doubtless there is much room for improvement still. I find that the case with myself; and I have been trying to be a good girl a much longer time than you have. But, Lucy," she added, seriously, detaining the little girl a moment, "if you really wish to be good, you must ask the help of your heavenly Father to make you so. Ask him to put his Spirit in your heart and make you love him. That is the only way to be good and happy, in this world or the next. Now go and take your ride, and see how many pleasant things you will have to tell me when you come home."

"I don't believe any one in the world is so good as my cousin Deborah," said Lucy to Anne.

Lucy was mounted on her good, patient little donkey, and, with Anne at her side, was riding down the avenue towards the lodge beside the great gate. The old trees, of which there was a double row on each side, met over her head; and the rooks, which had had their nests for a hundred years and more in the great elms, were apparently giving a great deal of good advice to their young ones in the branches. On either side stretched the park; and Lucy could see the deer resting in the fern, or bounding away as they approached. It was a lovely afternoon in August: the air was full of pleasant sounds and scents; and everywhere Lucy's eyes rested upon something beautiful.

"I do believe my cousin Deborah is the very best and kindest lady in the whole world," repeated Lucy. "Don't you think so, Anne?"

"Well, I do not think you will find many better, my lady," replied Anne. "This is not much like the way you were spending the afternoon five weeks ago this very day. Do you remember how that was?"

"Why, no," said Lucy, considering. "Oh, yes: I do, indeed," she added, shuddering. "Oh, Anne, how dreadful that was!"

"And you little thought who was coming to your rescue: did you?" continued Anne. "I am sure my heart was in my mouth when Madam

Burgess took me into the library, and there sat the parson and that fine gentleman in the gold-laced coat and waistcoat."

"I am sure it was very good in you, Anne," said Lucy. "I shall never forget it. But, oh, that unlucky thimble! I would give any thing if it was found, or if I had never touched it! It makes me feel so ashamed when Cousin Deborah praises me, and says and does such kind things! When Aunt Bernard scolded me, I did not feel so; I felt vexed and angry, and just like being revenged upon her; but I don't feel so now."

"Didn't Mrs. Corbet say any thing about the thimble this morning?" asked Anne.

"No: I don't think she has missed it yet. But, when she does, what shall I ever do or say?"

"It, is very unlucky, and that is the truth," said Anne. "I don't doubt that the beggar-woman got it; or perhaps a magpie spied it and took it away. If we could only find out where it was gone! If there were only a wise woman, now, like the one my aunt went to about her mistress's silver spoons!"

"What do you mean by a Wise woman, Anne?"

"Oh, a woman that can tell all sorts of things,—how to cure cattle, and how to find things that are lost or stolen. There was such a woman in Stanton-Corbet once; but Parson Burgess would not let her practise her arts there. He said she was a deceiver and an im———— What was the word, now?"

"An impostor?" said Lucy.

"Yes, an impostor. He preached a sermon about it, more by token it did not do much good, for the people went to her just the same: so, finally, he drove her away out of the parish."

"Did he say it was wicked to go to such people?"

"Yes, I believe so. I was young then, and didn't mind so much about sermons. But here we are at the lodge."

Lucy displayed her treasures, and had the pleasure of seeing one of the pretty little twin-girls dressed in the clothes she had brought, and also of being flattered and praised for her goodness and condescension.

Till Anne said,—"Now, Mary Bolton, don't you be turning the child's head, and making her think she is an angel all complete, just for such a little matter as that. I don't deny, it was kind in my little lady to work for your baby; but it is no more than she ought to do, seeing how much Mrs. Corbet does for her. Come, Lady Lucy; we must be on our way, if we are going to the village."

"Are you going across the common?" asked Mary Bolton. "You had better take the path through the plantation, I think. The gipsies on the common, and my little lady might be frightened."

"Gipsies?" asked Lucy, looking a little scared.

"Yes; and a wild lot they do look, to be sure. They say the old women are witches; and all the girls in the village are agog to have their fortunes told."

"Don't you be scared, Lady Lucy," said Anne. "They won't meddle with us, I dare say. By your leave, Mary Bolton, I would rather go across the common than the other way. I should not relish meeting any of those gentry in the woods. Betty Henwife will have to look sharp after her fowls, and the gamekeeper for his pheasants, now we have gipsies in the neighbourhood."

"Anne," said Lucy, after they had gone a little way, "do you suppose the gipsy-woman could tell me what has become of my mother's thimble?"

"I was just thinking of that very thing," returned Anne. "I should not wonder if she could; for they do tell wonderful things,—that is certain. See, there they are,—tents, donkeys, and all."

There they were, forming a picturesque group enough, with their ragged tents pitched under the shade of some old hawthorns, their donkeys and ponies tethered near by, and their kettle, boiling, suspended on sticks over the fire, with a tall old woman in a red cloak, just removing the cover and stirring the mess.

Half a dozen half-naked children lay about; and no sooner did they catch sight of Lucy than up they all jumped and ran towards her and Anne, begging vociferously. Another woman, still taller and older than the first, came striding towards them.

And Anne, calling to her, bade her call off the children, and the dogs, which were now adding their voices to the chorus.

"Don't you be frightened, my pretty little lady," said the old woman, in a coaxing voice. "No one shall hurt my pretty dear. She will cross the old gipsy's hand with silver, and see what a fine fortune I will tell her."

Lady Lucy and Anne looked at each other.

"Oh, yes; I know all about it," said the gipsy, nodding in a mysterious manner. "I know there is a fine gentleman at the wars whom she loves. And I know she has lately escaped from bondage and cruel oppressors, and all that has happened to her since."

Lucy and Anne again exchanged glances of awe and wonder,—both of them forgetting that this gipsy-woman could easily have learned all this from the gossip of the village.

And Lucy half whispered, "Do you suppose she could tell about the thimble?"

The gipsy-woman, like many other impostors of her class, had quick ears and quick wits. She caught the word "thimble," and easily guessed that Lucy had lost something of that sort.

"I can tell what has happened lately, too," she continued, in a mysterious tone. "I can see what is lost, and where it lies, shining like silver and gold, fit for a lady's finger when she is working for her true lover. Only cross the poor gipsy's hand with silver, and you shall see. As for you," she added, looking at Anne with a penetrating glance, "you have lately had a rise in life, and shall soon have another and there is a stout lad abroad at the wars who shall bring home a gold ring some day."

"Just hear that!" said Anne, turning pale. "How could she know any thing about John Martin, that went away to the wars with my lord?"

By this time Lady Lucy and Anne were prepared to believe any nonsense the gipsy chose to tell them.

And Lucy whispered, "Ask her about the thimble."

"My lady has lost—" began Anne.

But the woman cut her short. "I know; I know. She has lost a thimble. And, if she wants to find it, let her come to-morrow to the spring by the brook, and bring something which has lain by the thimble,—something of silver if it was silver, and of gold if it was gold,—and she shall know all she desires. But let her beware how she deceives or trifles with the gipsy-woman, lest she rue the day she saw me under the hawthorn tree."

Terrified by this threat, all the more alarming from its mystery, and by the frown and glance of the old woman, Lucy tremblingly promised all she required.

"Must it be something out of the same box?" she asked.

"Yes, out of the same box. Don't fail to let it be of the same metal, or it will do no good. Now, young woman, let me see your hand."

The gipsy told Anne a fine fortune, and sent her off greatly pleased. Lucy, however, was not so well satisfied. She knew instinctively that Cousin Deborah would never let her go to meet the gipsy-woman, and that she must do so by stealth, if at all. Here was a new labyrinth of deceit opening upon her.

"Oh, what a tangled web we weave
 When first we practise to deceive!"

These lines were not written in Lady Lucy's day, or she might have remembered them. She had made a resolution that she would never tell another lie; but what was to become of that resolution now? And what was it but stealing, if she took something else out of the box? But, then, if she did not? Lucy shuddered. She was timid by nature, and still more by education; and the thought of the gipsy's threats made her tremble and turn cold.

It is to be hoped that almost any little girl of the present day would have more sense than to be influenced as Lucy was. And yet I am not sure that one could not find both children and grown-up people doing quite as foolish things as going to a gipsy-woman about a lost thimble. Indeed, if there can be said to be any sense in the matter, there would seem to be two or three grains more in going to a live woman for information than in asking a dead table.

But Lucy had never been taught any better: indeed, what teaching she had ever received on the subject had been the other way.

You may easily see how Lady Lucy was prepared to fall into the snare which the gipsy-woman had laid for her. She no more doubted that the woman could tell where the thimble was, than she doubted that she had lost it. And she felt more and more that she would give any thing she had to get it into her own possession again: first, because, despite Cousin Deborah's kindness, she could not divest herself of the idea that she should be severely punished if it were known that she had lost it; and secondly, because she could not bear to part with the thimble her dear mamma had used when a little girl like herself.

That the gipsy might impose upon her, or that, even if she found out where the thimble was, she might not be able to get it back again, were matters which she never thought of. Her whole mind was occupied with contriving how she might get down to the spring to-morrow without the knowledge of Cousin Deborah. And she arrived at home before she had come to any satisfactory decision.

# CHAPTER IV.

"THE post-boy have been here and brought some letters," said Jenny, as she met Lucy in the hall. "I should not wonder if Mrs. Corbet had news of my lord your father. Anyhow, you were to go to her as soon as you came in. She is sitting in the library."

Lucy would have found it hard to say whether she were most alarmed or delighted with this news. She walked very soberly through the gallery, where the portraits of all the long-dead Stantons and Corbets hung against the wall, with suits of armour and groups of strange weapons suspended between them, and tapped softly at the half-open library door.

"Come in, my love," answered Cousin Deborah's cheery voice, in a tone which removed some, at least, of Lucy's fears. "See, here is a treasure for you,—a letter from your dear father, and directed to yourself."

"Really for me, Cousin Debby?" asked Lucy, looking at the direction, and then turning the letter over and examining the broad seal. "I never had a letter of my own in my life."

"Really for you; and I hope you will appreciate your father's goodness in taking so much pains for you. I assure you I was twice—yes, three times—as old as you before I ever had a letter of my own. But open it, and let us hear the news. I did not examine it, because I thought you would like the pleasure of breaking the seal yourself."

"Just the way," thought Lucy. "She always thinks of what I shall like. Oh, how wicked I am! Oh, if I only dared tell her all about the thimble! I wonder if I could? But, then, the gipsy-woman, and those terrible threats. Oh, dear! I never thought I could be so unhappy at Stanton Court."

Lucy broke the seal of the letter neatly, as Cousin Deborah showed her how to do, and opened the broad sheet, which was closely written from end to end.

"Please to read it for me, Cousin Debby. I never can read writing-hand fast."

"You must take pains to learn, Lucy. I have some very pretty letters, which you can practise upon; but I will read this one to you, if you please."

The letter was dated at the Duke of Marlborough's head-quarters, near Neuburg, a little place on the river Danube, not very far from Ingolstadt. It gave an account of such events of his journey as Lord Stanton thought would be interesting to his little daughter.

"It is generally believed that we are upon the eve of a great and decisive battle," said he; "though exactly when and how it will take place, of course, I cannot inform you; but I believe before this letter reaches you, the Duke of Marlborough and his noble ally, Prince Eugene, will have defeated the army of the French king, under Marshall Tallard, or will have been defeated themselves. The soldiers are in the best of spirits, and full of trust in their great commander, insomuch that no officer thinks of asking the reason of any of his motions, but all follow him with blind confidence in his wisdom.

"But let my dear child give God thanks that she lives in a country where the horrors of such war are unknown. The sights one sees here are enough to break a man's heart. Smoking ruins which only a few days since were thriving towns and lovely hamlets; old men, and little children, and mothers with infants at their breasts, lying down to starve at the roadside, or killed by the falling of their own roof-trees; fruitful fields, lately ripening to the harvest, now trampled and bare: these are but a few of the horrors which constantly meet one's eyes. I do not suppose this ruin can be helped; but it is indeed hard that such distress and destruction should fall upon innocent heads, and that the French king, whose mad ambition has brought about all this, should be living in luxury and quietness, far from the very sound of war.

"It may be, my daughter, that this is the last letter you will ever receive from your father. The duke has bestowed upon me the command of my old regiment; and should there be a battle, which seems imminent, you may be sure that your father will not be backward to do his part and sustain the honour of our country. Should I fall, you will be left in a position of great responsibility. Never forget, my child, that you are but the steward of your wealth, which you are to use not for your own selfish ease and pleasure, but for the honour of God and the good of your fellows, specially of those who as tenants and servants are more immediately in your power and under your influence. Take your cousin Deborah's advice in all things, and be governed by her; but, above all, pray to your Father in heaven for the guidance of his Holy Spirit.

"These are matters which I have neglected too much in the course of my life; but during my imprisonment, and while I was deprived of all outward solace, God was pleased to bring me to a better mind; and I trust, if my life be spared, I shall serve him henceforth as a Christian man should do.

"One thing more, my dear Lucy: I parted with your aunt Bernard, as you know, in great anger,—not without just cause. But it is my duty to pardon all, even as I would myself be pardoned. I would not appear before God save in charity with all men. I therefore desire that you will convey to my sister Bernard the assurance of my full and free forgiveness, in such way as Cousin Deborah may think best; and I also desire that you, Lucy, will forgive her for the wrongs she has done you. Cease not to pray for your father, my child; and may the God of the fatherless be your support if I am taken from you!"

Lucy listened to this letter with quiet tears rolling down her face and dropping in Cousin Deborah's apron.

"Oh," she thought, "if I only dared tell her all about the thimble! If only it were not for those dreadful things the woman spoke of!"

"Now, Lucy, how shall we manage to convey your father's message to Aunt Bernard?" asked Cousin Deborah. "Will you go and carry it to her?"

"Oh, Cousin Deborah, I dare not!" said Lucy, turning pale. "I dare not speak to Aunt Bernard. You don't know how afraid I am of her."

Cousin Deborah put her arm round Lucy, and felt that she was trembling at the very idea of facing her aunt. A feeling of indignation crossed her mind as she thought what the tyranny must have been, which so affected the child that the mere notion of speaking to Mrs. Bernard was dreadful to her. She forbore to urge Lucy any further.

"Suppose, then, Lucy, you copy this message of your father's in your own handwriting, and add some words of your own. I think that will be the best course. And, my dear, I am sure you will not forget, in your own secret prayers, to beseech God's protection for your dear father in the perils to which he is exposed."

"Do you suppose there has been a battle, Cousin Deborah?" asked Lucy.

"Of course I cannot tell, my love. You see, your father himself did not know. Great generals are not accustomed to tell their plans until they are ready to act; and I have heard that the Duke of Marlborough is remarkable for keeping his own counsel. But, even if there has been no battle, your father may be in danger. Many soldiers are slain who are not killed in battle."

"Then perhaps my papa may be dead already," said Lucy. "Oh, Cousin Deborah, suppose I should be an orphan even now!" And Lucy burst into tears, and wept bitterly.

"My dearest child," said Cousin Deborah, taking Lucy upon her lap, and wiping away the tears which fell from her own eyes, "we cannot tell what may have happened; but, Lucy, you must try to remember that God is in Bavaria as well as here, and to trust in him to take care of your dear father. 'God is love,' you know St. John says in the verses we read this morning."

"But God will not love me, because I am a naughty girl," sobbed Lucy. "Aunt Bernard said God hated me and would send his judgments to destroy me."

"My dear child, never, never believe that God hates you,—no, not even if you feel that you have been ever so naughty," said Cousin Deborah. "He sent his dear Son to die for us because we were sinners, and for no other reason. It was therefore we stood in need of his death, because we were sinners. Sinner though you may be, God still loves you, and desires that you may repent and return to him; and the moment you do so, he is ready to receive and forgive you and treat you as his dear child once more. Sometimes our heavenly Father sees fit to punish his children, and so he sends some trouble upon them, even upon those who are trying to follow him the most faithfully; but that is no sign he does not love them, any more than it would be a sign I did not love you because I saw reason to reprove you for some fault. Will you remember this, my child?"

"Yes, Cousin Debby," whispered Lucy, hiding her face on her cousin's breast.

"Now, I want to talk to you about something else, Lucy," said Cousin Deborah, after a little silence. "I have received a letter from my cousin Paulina, who, you know, lives in Exeter and keeps a girls' school. She wishes me to come and see her, that she may advise with me about some matters of importance connected with her present enterprise. There are some reasons why I do not wish to take you at present; though I mean you shall go with me some day. And, if I leave you at home, will you be very steady, and do all your tasks, and be obedient to Anne?"

"I will try, Cousin Debby."

"I shall be gone a day or two,—not longer, I think," continued Cousin Deborah. "And if I hear a good account of you on my return, and see that you have tried to give me pleasure by being faithful and industrious, I shall be very much gratified; because it will show that you are a trustworthy little girl."

"Yes, Cousin Debby," murmured Lucy, again.

"Very well, my love. Then I shall venture to take this little journey, having confidence that you will not fall into any mischief because I am not here to watch you. I trust you, Lucy."

"When shall you go, Cousin Deborah?" asked Lucy, feeling—oh, so small and mean in her own estimation, as the thought crossed her mind that Cousin Deborah's going away would remove all hindrances to her meeting the gipsy-woman.

"I cannot tell until I see Mattison and find out what horse there is for me to ride. It is something of a journey,—twenty good miles; and I am not so good a horsewoman as I was thirty years ago, when I rode from Exeter to London on the mare that all the men were afraid of."

Mattison was an old, broken-down trooper, who was head-groom and general master of the horse at Stanton Court. Consultation with him revealed the fact that there was a steady old gray horse, just the thing for a lady like Mrs. Corbet, and a broken-down charger left behind by my lord, which would answer very well for Mattison, who was to accompany her. So it was settled that they should take an early breakfast and set out from Stanton Court in the cool of the morning, resting, during the hottest part of the day, at the house of an old lady, a friend of Cousin Deborah's.

Anne was a little surprised, the next morning, to see Lady Lucy, after she had watched her cousin down the avenue, turn into the terrace parlour, as it was called, and seat herself at her lute, with the hour-glass by which she was used to time her tasks, on the table by the side of her lesson-book. She had expected to see Lucy take the opportunity to play.

"You are very industrious, my lady," said she. "That is not the way you used to do when Mrs. Bernard went away."

"Aunt Bernard was one person, and Cousin Deborah is another," said Lucy. "Cousin Deborah said she trusted me to be a good girl; and I am going to try and please her. Aunt Bernard never trusted me; and you know yourself, Anne, I never could please her, do what I would. It never made one bit of difference whether I did my tasks or let them alone; and so I used to feel as though I might as well do one thing as an other. But Cousin Deborah always praises me if I do well and if I do ill, she does not seem vexed—only sorry; that makes me feel as though I wanted to do every thing right."

"Well, I'll not say but you are in the right," replied Anne, seriously. "Mrs. Corbet is one of the best ladies I ever knew, I will say for her; and it was a blessed day for you which put you into her hands. By the way, has she ever said any thing about the thimble?"

"Not a word," replied Lucy. "It seems as though she must have missed it; but she has never spoken about it."

"I don't understand it," returned Anne. "She may be waiting to see if you will find it and put it back of your own accord."

"Do you think the gipsy-woman will be able to tell where it is, Anne?"

"I can't justly say. They do know wonderful things, to be sure. And it is not safe to offend them, either; for there is no knowing what revenge they may take. There was a woman my grandmother knew, who lived on the edge of Exmoor,—" And forthwith Anne plunged into a foolish tale, effectually diverting Lucy's mind from her practising, and making her feel more than ever afraid of not keeping her appointment with the gipsy.

"If I could only feel right about Cousin Deborah," said she; "but I am almost sure she will not like it."

"She will not know it," argued Anne; "and what folks don't know don't hurt them, folks say."

"I don't know I think it does, sometimes," said Lucy. "But, anyhow, I cannot help feeling mean and wicked when Cousin Deborah talks about trusting me and I know that I am telling her lies and deceiving her all the time. I wish I had told her all about the thimble the first minute I lost it. If I had gone out and picked it up, and told her how it came out there, she might have been angry; but she would have forgiven me, I know, and it would have been all right now."

"Then why did you not tell her before she went away?" asked Anne.

"That was different," replied Lucy. "I had told her more than one lie already; and you know how she hates lies. And there is the gipsy-woman, too! But please, Anne, don't talk to me any more now. I want to practise my music and learn my tables, as I promised Cousin Deborah."

Dinner-time came, and near the hour at which they had promised to meet the gipsy, Lucy and Anne were at the spring. The woman was there before them, seated on a stone, with her red cloak drawn about her, and her elbow resting on her knee. She was stirring the water of the little spring with a peeled rod she held in her hand, and seemed to be muttering something to herself.

"So you are come at last," said the hag, sternly, addressing herself to Lucy. "Well for you that you were no later. Have you brought what I told you?"

Lucy trembled as she drew from her pocket a small, gold-handled fruit-knife and put it into the hand of the woman, whose experienced eyes at once told her that the metal was pure.

"It is small; but it may do," said she. She turned her back upon the two spectators, and proceeded to rub the knife, to breathe upon it, and go through various mystical ceremonies, while Lucy and Anne looked on in silent awe.

"You must leave this with me to-night," she said; "and to-morrow at this hour you must bring me something more."

"I must not,—I dare not," exclaimed Lucy, in great distress.

"But you shall," said the witch, with a fearful frown, "or great trouble will visit you. Take your choice; but remember." And, without another word, she turned her back upon Lucy and Anne, and stalked off down the valley by the side of the brook, till a turn in the path hid her from their eyes.

# CHAPTER V.

"WELL, my lady," said Anne, when the old woman had disappeared, "what shall we do now?"

Lucy stood looking at the spring, watching the tiny stream as it trickled down the rock and fell, with a soft, silver tinkle, into the little stone basin. She stood a while in silence, and her face began to assume a new expression,—a look of gentle determination, such as Anne had never seen upon it before.

"What shall we do, my lady?" repeated Anne.

And at the same moment, Jack, the donkey, who had stood patiently dozing during the whole interview, pushed his head over Lucy's shoulder.

"We will go home," said Lucy, lifting her eyes from the spring at last; "and we will never come here again,—never!" she repeated, firmly.

"Hush, for mercy's sake, my dear child!" whispered Anne. "You don't know who may be listening to you. There! Did you hear that?" she added, starting, as a strange sound, something like a laugh, was heard over their heads.

Lucy looked up. "It is the carrion crow. Don't you see him up on the dead tree yonder?"

"The corby! Oh, my lady, what will become of us? They say he is always a messenger of ill."

"Ill or well, I will not come here again nor will I give that woman any more of my dear mother's things. Come, Anne; put me on the donkey, and let us go home."

Anne obeyed, wondering what had come over her young lady. She would have gone on talking about the corby; but Lucy stopped her.

"Don't,—please, Anne. I want to think about something."

Presently they met Dr. Burgess, striding along the path, with a stick in his hand, and humming a psalm-tune.

"Heyday, whom have we here? My little Lady Lucy, as I am alive! And what are you doing in this lonely place, my love?"

"My lady came out for a ride, and wished to see the spring," Anne replied, readily enough.

"Ay, 'tis a curious solitary place: is it not, my dear? There are many such in these Devonshire coombs; and some day, if Mrs. Corbet will kindly give us permission, I will take you and my own girls to see a very beautiful spring in Ferncoomb, where there are the remains of an ancient chapel and hermitage. 'Tis a treat I have long promised to Polly and Dulcie. Meantime, Lady Lucy, I would advise you to take your rides and walks in more frequented places. These gipsies are a lawless gang, and I would not have you encounter them. They are making mischief in the parish, stealing fowls and fruit, and turning the girls' heads with their fortune-telling nonsense. I hear they have fooled Dame Shearer out of a good round sum, pretending to tell her where the money is her husband lost coming from the fair."

"Do you not think, then, that they can tell where it is?" Lucy gathered courage to ask.

"I think it not unlikely they may know where it is, but I doubt very much whether they will ever tell her," answered Dr. Burgess, drily.

He was silent for a few moments, and then asked Lucy if she had heard from her father since his departure.

Lucy told him she had just received a letter, and repeated what her father had said, in respect to the probability of a great battle.

"You will doubtless feel very anxious till you can hear again," said the doctor, kindly: "but, my dear child, strive to put your trust in God and rely upon his mercy and goodness. Doubtless you pray for your father every day, and we at the parsonage will add our petitions to yours."

"Dr. Burgess," said Lucy, presently, in a low voice, and raising her eyes timidly to the face of the good clergyman.

"Well, my daughter."

"Will you please to explain something to me?"

"Surely, surely, my daughter. I shall be glad to do so."

"My father says," continued Lucy, "that I must ask God for the guidance of his Holy Spirit. What does that mean?"

In plain and well-chosen words, Dr. Burgess explained to Lucy the meaning of the phrase. "It is your privilege and your duty to ask constantly for this guidance, my dear, young lady," he added. "But then, when you have received it, you must follow it."

"How can I tell when I have received it?" asked Lucy.

"Your conscience, and the word of God, must be your guide," replied Dr. Burgess. "When your conscience tells you that what you are about to do is wrong, you must obey its voice and refrain; and when it bids you do thus, and so you must obey also, no matter what it costs. Now, do you understand?"

"I think I do," replied Lucy. "Thank you, sir!"

"Is there any thing else I can do for you?" asked Dr. Burgess, kindly, as they came near the lodge. "Do not fear to ask me. There is nothing which pleases me more than to have the young people of my charge come to me for advice or assistance."

"I am sure, you are very good to me; every one is very good to me, I think," said Lucy. "I did not think there were such good people in the world."

"There are both good and bad in the world, as you will soon find,—as indeed I think you have found already," replied the good clergyman, smiling. "May God bless you, my child, and give you his grace in every time of need."

Lucy took in her own little fingers the broad hand the doctor laid upon her head and kissed it.

"I love you dearly," she whispered. "You will pray for my dear father, and for me, too?"

"Indeed, I will," said the doctor; "and so will we all. Farewell, and be a good girl, and do not stir far from home while your good cousin is away. Home is the safest place for little maids, gentle or simple."

"I am going up to my room, Anne," said Lucy, as she entered the door. "Please to call me when my supper is ready."

"What has got into that child?" said Anne to herself, gazing after Lucy as she ascended the broad staircase. "She looks the very moral of my lord, her father. I never thought of it before."

And Anne, who, like others of her class, delighted in prophecies of evil, pursed up her mouth, and talked so mysteriously and dolefully in the kitchen, that the little scullion maid was not a little perplexed.

When Anne went up to call Lady Lucy to supper, she found her reading her Bible—her own mother's velvet-bound and golden-clasped Bible—which her father had given her before she went away.

"This Bible," he said, "cost your dear mother her home and friends, and many a tear besides; and yet it was the greatest treasure of her heart. Be sure you prize it as she did, and make it the rule of your life."

Afterwards Cousin Deborah told Lucy the outline of her mother's story. She had belonged to a Protestant family in the south of France, on the border of Italy; but her own father and mother dying when she was eight or nine years old, she had been adopted by an aunt. This aunt had abandoned the Protestant principles, for which so many of her ancestors had perished upon the wheel and at the stake, and had become a Roman Catholic of the strictest school. She had done her best to bring up the little Lucille in the same way. But Lucille always remembered, and secretly clung to, the faith she had learned at her dead mother's knee. Perhaps, too, the strictness and gloom of her aunt did not tend to make the young girl in love with her religion.

At any rate, when she was eighteen, she fell in with one of the Protestant preachers, who had been a friend of her parents; was instructed by him more fully in their faith, and more than once attended their secret meetings. And being finally threatened with lifelong imprisonment in a convent, she had joined herself to one of the families of the Huguenot refugees, who were leaving France by hundreds at that time. And, after many perils, arrived safely in London, where Lord Stanton, then a young soldier, met, fell in love with, and married her. This English Bible had been his first gift to his bride, and dearly did Lucy love it for her mother's sake. For her sake, too, she had read it every day since her father put it into her hands; but now she was studying it for her own.

Lucy looked up from her book as Anne entered the room. She had been weeping, and the tears still hung on her long, curved eyelashes but her face wore a new expression of peace and happiness.

She was very silent for the rest of the evening, and did not seem disposed to listen to Anne's gossip as usual, but sat knitting on the stocking which she had begun the day before, now and then glancing at the Bible which lay open before her at the ninety-first Psalm.

Anne thought she was getting it by heart.

"How loud the sea roars!" said Lucy. "I haven't heard it so loud since we came here."

"There is going to be a storm," replied Anne. "See there is a flash already! Mercy on me, Lady Lucy! What shall we do if there is a thunderstorm?"

"Wait till it is over, I suppose," said Lucy, "and pray that we may be taken care of."

"Well, I know one thing," said Anne. "I wish that you had not angered that woman. I cannot get her face out of my mind."

"Dr. Burgess is not afraid of her, you see," said Lucy. "He called her an impostor, and said he meant to drive her out of the parish. I will have nothing more to do with her; of that I am resolved, come what will."

"Then you will lose the knife as well as the thimble," said Anne: "and what will your cousin say to that?"

"I fear she will be very angry, but I cannot help that," replied Lucy. "I am not going to do any more wrong things if I can help it. One lie just leads to another, and so on, till there is no end to them."

"I should just like to know what has set you on thinking of all these grave things so suddenly," said Anne. "You never did so at Mrs. Bernard's, and you read six chapters in the Bible, for one that you read with Mrs. Corbet."

"That was very different," said Lucy. "Aunt Bernard never explained any thing to me. All she did was to slap my hands if I did not call the words right; and she kept me standing up to read till I was ready to drop, and so stupid that I could not understand any thing if I tried. Cousin Deborah only lets me read a short lesson at a time,—one psalm, or a part of a chapter, in the New Testament,—and she explains every verse, and tells me the meaning of all the hard words. It was one verse we talked about which made me resolve to have nothing more to do with the gipsy, and to confess the truth to Cousin Debby when she comes home."

"Tell me all about it," said Anne, willing to talk about any thing rather than hold her tongue and listen to the approaching thunder, and the roar of the waves on the beach below. "What was the verse?"

"It was, 'If I regard wickedness in my heart, the Lord will not hear me!'" repeated Lucy. "Cousin Deborah said that meant that if we kept wicked thoughts in our minds, and wicked desires in our hearts, God would not hear our prayers. She said that we need not be afraid to pray, even though we had been ever so wicked, if only we were truly sorry for our sin; but unless we were sorry, and meant to leave off our sin, there was no use in praying."

"True enough," said Anne, in rather a sleepy tone. "My! What a flash. The storm is coming nearer and nearer."

"Well," continued Lucy, "then came the letter from my dear father, in which he said they were going to have a dreadful battle, and asked me to pray to God for him. I do want to pray for him," said Lucy, with a trembling voice. "It seems to be all the comfort there is, when I think of him in the midst of the swords and cannon balls, or perhaps lying on the ground wounded under the horses' feet, like that poor soldier in the great picture down-stairs: but what is the use of my praying, if I am inclining to wickedness with my heart all the time?"

"These are grave thoughts for a little lady like you," said Anne, not altogether at ease in her own mind. "I am sure the parson could not say all that any better. I don't like filling a young head with such things, for my part. Time enough when you grow an old lady, like Mrs. Corbet."

"Perhaps I shall never live to be an old lady like Mrs. Corbet," said Lucy: "and the French soldiers will not wait for me to grow up, to shoot at my dear papa."

"And that is true, too," said Anne. "Well, my dear, I am sure I am glad you find comfort in the Bible, and I would be the last one to oppose you. I remember when my poor sister was in the waste of which she died; after her sweetheart was drowned in the fishing-boat, the Bible was her only comfort. I have been sorry ever since, that I let you have any thing to do with that gipsy-woman; and I shall never forgive myself if harm comes of it to you."

"What harm can come besides the loss of the knife and of my silver sixpence? I do not believe the Lord will hear that wicked woman,—for I am sure she is wicked,—and you know, Anne, if he takes care of us, nothing can harm us. I was learning a beautiful psalm this very evening which tells about that. Shall I say it to you?"

Anne assented; and Lady Lucy repeated the ninety-first psalm. Long before it was finished, Anne was sound asleep. And Lucy, notwithstanding the thunder, lightning, and rain, soon followed her example.

When she opened her eyes, it was broad daylight. The sun was shining, and a dear little robin-redbreast was singing his song right on her window-seat. Lucy slipped out of bed and went to the window. Every thing was drenched and dripping with wet. It had evidently blown hard during the night, for in more than one place, broken branches were hanging on the trees or lying on the grass: but every thing glittered in the sunlight, the air was fresh and sweet, and the world seemed to be rejoicing in the new light of morning.

Thankful tears rose to Lucy's eyes, and she repeated the words of her morning hymn:—

"Glory to Him who safe hath kept,
 And hath preserved me while I slept;
 Grant, Lord, when I from death shall wake,
 I may of endless life partake."

She stole softly to the door and opened it a little way. There lay a friend indeed, no less than Goodman, the old bloodhound, who had been a puppy when her father went away, and had known him again when he came back. Old Goodman who was allowed to go about as he liked, and who had more than once hidden himself in the house and stayed all night in some snug corner. He now lay comfortably snoozing on the mat, but lifted his head and knocked his tail against the floor as Lucy opened the door.

"You dear, faithful, old dog," said Lucy, bending over him and patting the great head tenderly. "Did you come to take care of your little mistress, you dear dog? You shall have some of my breakfast and sleep here every night till Cousin Deborah comes home. And you will take care of your little mistress, won't you, old fellow?"

Goodman lazily put up his tawny muzzle and licked Lucy's face, as if ratifying this treaty on his own part. And Lucy, feeling her heart lighter than for many a day, went back to her room to dress.

"Dear me, Lady Lucy, are you up already?" asked Anne, sleepily. "I am sure it is very early."

"It is six o'clock and a beautiful morning," replied Lucy, adding rather mischievously: "I should think you had slept sound enough, Anne. You never heard the storm last night. And, Anne, go down and see about my breakfast. I should like to be alone a little while."

All that day Lucy kept herself closely within the limits of the house and garden, doing her task with punctilious accuracy. She even resumed the open-hem ruffling which had lain untouched in her drawer ever since she came from Aunt Bernard's, intending to ask Cousin Deborah if she might make it into something for the twins at the lodge, in which she took a great interest. She would have liked to go down and see the dear little babies, but she thought it likely enough that she might encounter the gipsy-woman, and she wisely judged it best to keep out of her way.

The old bloodhound, her self-elected guardian, was faithful to his trust, stalking up and down the terrace at Lucy's side, sitting at her elbow at meal-times, and lying at her feet while she was reading or working in the terrace parlour. There was nothing very remarkable in the dog's taking a fancy to the lonely little girl, who had always a kind word for him in passing and often gave him a share of the bun, or the bit of ginger-bread which Cousin Deborah allowed her. Neither was it surprising, that Goodman should prefer lying on the Turkey carpet in the parlour to reposing upon the flags outside.

Nevertheless, Anne chose to see in it a new marvel, and pointed it out to Jenny with many significant shrugs and winks.

When Lucy went to bed, Goodman still accompanied her, and settled himself down on the mat in a composed matter-of-fact way, which moved Anne to say that the dog had more sense than some Christians.

There was another thunder-storm in the night, but Lucy only roused herself to wonder whether there were any fishermen out in their boats from the cove below; to murmur a prayer for them, and for her father and cousin and then sank to sleep again.

"Will Mattison has come home," was the news which met Lucy, as she came down-stairs the next morning. "He is waiting to speak to you."

"Has not my cousin come, then?" asked Lucy, her heart beating fast. "Oh, Anne, has any thing happened to Cousin Deborah?"

"Now, don't, my lady! I don't think any harm has come to Mrs. Corbet; but Will will tell you all about it. Shall I send him in to you?"

It turned out that nothing serious was the matter. Cousin Deborah had met an old friend in Exeter, who persuaded her to stay a night with her upon the road. And she had sent Will Mattison home with her parcels, that he might apprise Lady Lucy of the cause of her delay.

"I got to the village last night just as the storm came up," concluded Will: "so I thought it better to put up at the ale-house, rather than run the risk of spoiling my mistress' bundles of mercery. And, my lady, if I might presume to offer my advice, you will not stir outside the gardens and park while your cousin is away. I heard a deal of talk about the gipsies, down at the village last night. They say they are a desperate gang, and the very same that was chased out of Somersetshire this spring. Not as I believe all the nonsense folks tell about the gipsies either. I dare say there may be good and bad among them, but these here is a bad-looking set, surely, and it wouldn't be altogether pleasant for a young lady to meet with them. I hope you will excuse the freedom, my lady—"

"You are quite right, Will, and I thank you for your care of me. You see I have one guard already," added Lucy, patting the head of the old dog. "Now go and tell cook to give you a good breakfast."

"I never did see any one so changed as my young lady," said Will, as he returned to the kitchen. "When she first came here, she was as scared as a young fawn, and the moment any one spoke to her, her great black eyes were looking every way like a startled hares: but now she seems to have plucked up a spirit, and speaks so quiet and dignified like. That old woman must have used the child awful to have cowed and broken her spirit so. It makes my old blood boil to think of it."

Lucy ate her breakfast with old Goodman sitting at her elbow contentedly munching the crusts she gave him. Then she walked a while upon the terrace; visited and inspected a litter of kittens which Will had found in the stable; and finally sat down to her lessons in the bow-window, with the dog still in close attendance.

She had finished her practising and learned her spelling-lesson, and was sitting industriously working at the open-hem she used to dislike so much, when the window was suddenly darkened by a shadow, and, at the same moment, Goodman bristled up and gave a deep growl.

Lucy looked up.

There before the open window stood the gipsy-woman, with her black glittering eyes fixed upon Lucy's face.

"So, my young lady, this is the way you keep your promise to the gipsy-woman! You bring me to the place appointed and keep me waiting, the whole afternoon while you take your pleasure at home. But beware what you do! I am not to be played with, as you may find to your cost some day."

For the moment, Lucy's fears overmastered her new-found faith and courage. She sat pale and trembling, unable to stir or even to call for help. The wicked woman saw her advantage.

"Did you hear the storm last night and the night before? Ay, but did you know what was riding upon the lightning and the wind, waiting only for my word to lay this proud roof-tree and all beneath it low in the dust? You little know what my art can do yet for good or evil!"

She fixed her eyes upon the work-box which stood open on the table, and continued, in a still fiercer tone, "Give me something from that box as I bade you; give me my choice from it, and you shall find all you have lost, and be lucky and prosperous henceforth. Refuse or betray me, and you shall never know one peaceful night more, but shall pine and pine, till you shall wish in vain for death to release you. Give it me, I say, or I will take it."

"I will not!" returned Lucy, finding her voice and her courage all at once. "You are a wicked woman; and I will not give you any more of my dear mother's things. Goodman, watch good dog!"

The woman made a stride forward, and stretched out her hand towards the box.

Goodman seemed to think the time had come for action. With a fearful growl, he sprang forward in his turn, and would have caught her by the throat.

But, luckily for her, a rough hand was laid upon her shoulder pulling her back, and a rough voice said,—

"Halloo, mistress! What are you about here, frightening my young lady? Down, Goodman, but watch. Be quiet, woman! The dog would as soon pull you down as a deer, if I gave him the word. What are you about, my lady, talking with such riff-raff?"

"Oh, Will Mattison, I am so glad you are come!" exclaimed Lucy, bursting into tears. "Oh, take her away!"

The woman smoothed her frowning brow and softened her tones wonderfully. "Nay, master, no need to be so rough. There is no harm done nor meant, only my little honey-sweet lady is so easily scared. If she would but listen a moment, she would hear the fine fortune I have to tell her."

"Coarse or fine, we want none of your fortunes: so you may just troop off," said Will, stoutly. "My lady, have you any thing to say to this woman?"

"No, oh, no! Take her away, but do not hurt her."

"Oh, I will go fast enough, never fear. No need to bid your man drive me away. I will go fast enough, never to return; and no more shall some one else, neither shall that which is lost ever be found again: mind that, my fair lady. Never again shall you find what you have lost or see your father's face. Yes, I will go; but, mayhap, I will send them in my place that shall make my scornful lady wish the old gipsy back again, but I shall be far away. Oh, yes, I will go."

"Go, then, and make us quit of you," said the sturdy old trooper, not at all alarmed at this mysterious threat. "I am too old a soldier to be scared at a woman's tongue, be she young or old. I've seen plenty of your sort in Germany and the low countries, where they use less ceremony with vagrants than here. Come, troop!"

"Oh, Will, don't anger her!" said Anne, who had come in and stood trembling at the scene. "Don't anger her. There's no knowing what she may do. What if she should curse you?"

"Let her," returned Will. "I will tell you, girl, a good saying I learned long ago from the Moors at Tangier; 'Curses are like young chickens, they always come home to roost.' I am a Christian man I trow, and shall I have less courage than a heathen Moor? Come, mistress; troop, I say!"

"Well, I do say it is a fine thing to travel abroad," said Anne, looking at Will as he followed the woman along the terrace. "Just hear how she is cursing him! I wouldn't be in his place for something."

"She is gone, my lady," said Will, presently reappearing at the bow-window. "I promise you she gave it to me finely. Such a foul mouth I never heard, even among the gipsies. But don't you fear her. I don't believe the good Lord is going to bring evil on this honourable house for any curses of hers. So don'tee cry any more, my dear young lady, don'tee now," continued the good old man, as Lucy's tears still fell fast upon the head of old Goodman, which he had laid on her knee; "but be a brave maid and all will be well. Goodman and old Will Mattison will take good care of you till Mrs. Corbet returns. And in good time here she comes," he added, looking towards the avenue. "I wonder what has brought her home so early in the day? Anyhow, I am glad to see her, and I must go and hold her horse. So wipe up your tears, there's a brave maid, and go to meet your cousin."

# CHAPTER VI.

"WHAT! Tears upon your cheeks, my Lucy," said Mrs. Corbet, as she dismounted from her horse and bent to kiss Lucy. "Nay, my child, that is but a sorry welcome."

"My lady has just been frightened by a gipsy-woman, and no shame to her," said Will Mattison. "She came to the window as bold as brass, when my lady was alone all but old Goodman, and a fearsome bold hag she was; but I sent her to the right about, I promise you. You have come earlier than I expected, madam."

"Yes; I had the offer of good company in the Vicar of Clevelay, who was riding this way, and I thought best to accept it. And so you had a fright, my love? I am sorry for that; but put it out of your mind now. No harm shall happen to you. Good old dog,—brave Goodman! Have you been taking care of Lucy?"

"Indeed he has, cousin! He has slept at my door every night since you went away, and he will not leave me a moment."

"Were you frightened at the thunder, Lucy?"

"I was the first night, but not the second," said Lucy. "I went to sleep in the midst of it."

"That was well. Now, come up with me in my room, while I take off my hat and habit."

There was a shade of anxiety and care under all Cousin Debby's cheery manner. The truth was, she had heard the report that there had been a great battle fought between the Duke of Marlborough's forces and those of the French king. It was no more than a rumour; but Cousin Debby well knew how apt such rumours are to prove true, and she wished to be at home with Lucy when any authentic news should arrive.

It was with a fluttering and sinking heart that Lucy followed her cousin along the gallery to her own room. She had fully determined to confess all her fault to Cousin Debby, whatever might be the consequence; nor did she swerve from her resolution as the time drew near for putting it into practice. Nevertheless, she trembled so violently that her limbs almost failed to support her, when she found herself alone with Mrs. Corbet in her own room.

If Cousin Deborah noticed her agitation, she probably imputed it to Lucy's late fright; for she made no remark upon it, but talked to Lucy of her journey, as she took off her riding-hat and bathed her face and hands.

Then, sitting down in her chair, she called the little girl to her side, and put into her hands a small case, which she took from her pocket.

"Open it, my dear! See, this is the way."

Lucy opened it, and started with surprise. There lay the missing thimble, in all its old beauty of blue and white enamel, the gold as bright and pure as ever, with her mother's name upon the side.

"Had you missed it?" asked Cousin Deborah. "I had an opportunity of sending to Exeter: so I despatched it to the goldsmith there to be mended and made a little smaller, that you might sometimes have the pleasure of using your mother's thimble. Why, Lucy, my dear child, what is the matter?"

For Lucy had dropped upon her knees by her cousin's side, and, hiding her face in her lap, was crying so bitterly, that her whole frame was convulsed by her sobs.

"Hush! Hush! My child. You will make yourself ill," said Cousin Deborah, soothing her. "What is it makes you cry? Did you think the thimble was lost?"

"Oh, Cousin Debby, I have been so wicked," sobbed Lucy. "You will never love me again, when I tell you what I have done."

"I shall not cease to love you, though you have been ever so naughty, if I see you are sorry for what you have done," said Cousin Deborah, gravely but kindly. "Compose yourself, my child, and tell me all about the matter."

In low tones, and often interrupted with sobs, Lucy confessed the whole, hiding nothing, and making no attempt to excuse herself.

Cousin Deborah listened in silence.

As Lucy finished her tale, she laid her head again upon her cousin's knee. She expected to feel herself lifted roughly to her feet, and shaken out of breath; but she seemed determined to keep hold of her refuge as long as possible.

But in a minute, a gentle hand stroked down her hair, and a gentle voice said,—

"My poor, little, weak-spirited girl! Could you not trust Cousin Deborah?"

Lucy's tears flowed fast once more, but they were very different tears.

"See how much harm has come from your cowardice," continued Cousin Deborah. "If you had told me directly you lost the thimble, I should have been displeased, indeed, at your disobedience, but there would have been the end. You would have been spared all this grief, and anxiety, and all the terrors you suffered from the gipsy-woman. You would not have lost your dear mother's knife, and, above all, Lucy, you would not have been tempted to tell so many lies."

"I kept thinking all the time that I would not tell any more," said Lucy; "but, somehow, they kept coming all the more."

"Yes, that is always the way. One lie leads to another, till we become involved in a web of deceit, and feel as if we knew not how to stir hand or foot. I am thankful you had the courage to break away at last."

"It was that verse about inclining unto wickedness that helped me more than any thing," said Lucy, gathering courage from her cousin's kindness. "I kept thinking how I could pray for papa, while I was being so naughty."

"Well," said Cousin Deborah, encouragingly, as Lucy paused, "what then?"

"I thought of it there at the spring, when the witch threatened that I should never see papa again unless I brought her something more," continued Lucy, "and that made me resolve I would never go again, whatever happened to me, and that I would tell you all about it."

Lucy went on to tell her cousin about her meeting and conversation with Dr. Burgess, and added, "I am not quite sure I did right, cousin, but when I came home, I shut myself up in my own room and prayed to God to forgive me, and give me his Holy Spirit, as the doctor said; and, Cousin Debby, was it wicked? It did really seem as if he heard me and gave me new strength and courage; and then I resolved again that I would tell all about it as soon as you came home. Was it really his guiding me by his Spirit, Cousin Deborah?" asked Lucy, in a tone of deep awe.

"I have not a doubt of it, my child."

"And you will forgive me, won't you, cousin?" pleaded Lucy. "Indeed, indeed, I am so very sorry!"

"I forgive you with all my heart, my dear," said Cousin Deborah, kissing her; "and I trust you will never be so foolish again as to be afraid of me. Now, I must send Will Mattison with a note to Dr. Burgess, if perhaps he may be able to do something towards recovering the knife. Stay you here, meanwhile, and we will talk of the matter again."

When Cousin Deborah returned, she took Lucy on her lap, and talked with her very seriously about the sin she had committed. Lucy was very penitent and very much ashamed; nevertheless, she felt happier than she had done in a long time. Cousin Deborah explained to her also the folly of supposing that God would reveal to an ignorant, wicked woman the things which were about to happen, or which had happened at a distance, and of thinking that he would allow such a person to harm his own children by enchantments or spells.

"But they do know things somehow," Lucy ventured to say, "or how could that woman have guessed it was a thimble I had lost?"

"Did not you and Anne say something about it?"

"I remember now I did tell Anne to ask her about the thimble," said Lucy, "and perhaps she overheard me. I remember, too, she did not know whether it was a silver or a gold thimble. Yet, if she had known where it was, she might have told what it was made of, one would think. But, Cousin Debby, she knew that my father was at the war, and that Jack Martin went with him."

"I dare say and so does every one in the village know it, and that Anne and Jack Martin were engaged to be married: so you see there is nothing wonderful in that. No doubt they pick up a great deal of such information which they use as occasion serves. Then, too, their tribes are scattered all over the world, and are said to keep up constant intercourse with one another: so they may often obtain news of what is passing abroad in a way which seems very wonderful to those not in the secret."

"Who are the gipsies, Cousin Deborah? They do not look like English people."

"It is not known from whence they came in the first place. They seem to have made their first appearance in Europe in the fifteenth century, (there were more than one hundred in Paris in 1427), and were then believed to have come from Egypt. Gipsy is from the French word Egyptien. There have been a great many speculations concerning them. * They evidently have a language and customs of their own. They are a great pest wherever they go, from their thieving, begging habits, and it may be doubted whether they are not often concerned in worse crimes."

* Mr. Grellmann supposes that they are of the lowest class of East Indians, viz., Pariahs, or Soodras, and that they were driven from Hindoostan to Europe, by Timur Beg, in 1408 or 1409.

"Why do not people try to teach them better, Cousin Deborah?"

"My dear, that is a question I have often asked myself. It does not seem to me that Christian people have awaked to their duty in that respect, and that something might be done for these wretched outcasts. Their unsettled mode of life, however, is much in the way of gaining any influence over them. And so long as they can make a subsistence by their pretended acts of fortune-telling and treasure-finding, they are not likely to settle to any honest employment.

"I hope, my dear Lucy, you will never be so foolish again as to go to these wretched people for any such purpose. And, now, tell me another thing, Lucy. Do you think it is a very pleasant thing for a little girl to have secrets which she is afraid will be found out by those who have the care of her?"

"No, indeed, Cousin Deborah! I hope I shall never have another secret as long as I live."

"I know," continued Cousin Deborah, "that the way in which you have hitherto been brought up has made you timid and reserved. You have always been so severely treated for every little fault and mishap, that you have fallen into the habit of concealing your faults, and even of lying to hide them. Now this is a very sad habit, and one of which you must take great pains to break yourself. It is cowardice, and leads to a great deal of meanness and wickedness."

"Yes, I know," said Lucy. "It made me tell lies about the thimble; and I did use to tell a great many to Aunt Bernard, I know; but, oh, Cousin Debby, if you knew how she used to punish me for the least little thing! She would not let me have one bit of drink with my meals for a whole week once, because I spilled some milk on my slip; and it was her speaking sharply to me that made me spill it, too. Oh, it did seem as if I should choke just eating dry crust for my breakfast and supper!" *

* A fact.

"I know all that, Lucy, and that has been an excuse for you heretofore; but it will be so no longer. I want you to feel, my child, how mean and wicked it is to tell a lie, whether it is to hide a fault or to escape punishment; and I wish you to have enough confidence in me to come to me in all your troubles great and small. Will you not try to do this?"

"Yes, Cousin Debby." Lucy Was silent for a few minutes, leaning on her cousin's breast. Then she said, softly, "Cousin!"

"Well, my love!"

"I should like to write out that piece of my father's letter for Aunt Bernard."

"You shall do so, Lucy. Do you not feel now that you can add some words of your own, telling poor Aunt Bernard that you forgive her for your own part?"

"Yes, Cousin Debby. I feel differently now. But, cousin, I don't think it would be true for me to say that I loved Aunt Bernard."

"You need not say so; but Lucy, can you not think of something for which you ought to beg Aunt Bernard's pardon? Did you not do some wrong things?"

"Yes, Cousin Debby, I know I did. What shall I write?"

"I shall not tell you what to say, Lucy. You shall write just what you think and feel, and show it to me afterwards, if you please. Here is paper, pens, and ink in my cabinet. You may sit down here and write, while I put away my habit and my other things."

Lucy was just sitting down to write, when, glancing out of a side-window, she exclaimed: "Oh, Cousin Debby, here comes Will Mattison galloping up the avenue as hard as he can pelt, and waving his hat. And all the church bells are ringing. Oh, what has happened?"

"I presume there is some news come from the war," said Cousin Debby. "Let us go down and see. Do not tremble so, my dearest child, but look up to your heavenly Father for strength."

"News! Madam and my lady! Great news from the war!" exclaimed Will, throwing himself from his smoking horse at the hall door. "There has been a great victory, and lord is safe and well! Here are letters come from him. The man who brought them rode post from London, and his horse was wearied out as well as himself."

"Thank God, my dear Lucy, your father is well!" said Cousin Deborah, glancing at the hurried note. "Sit down and hear what he says."

Lucy was glad to sit down, for her limbs trembled too much to support her. The letter was dated at Blenheim, the fourteenth day of August, 1704, and was as follows:—

"MY DEAREST DAUGHTER:—Yesterday being Sunday, the thirteenth day of August, 1704, was fought the most dreadful battle I have ever yet seen, resulting in a complete victory on our part over the French and their allies. The carnage on both sides has been dreadful, but we have suffered much less than the French. I have got off with a sabre cut on my forehead, which is no great matter, but will not improve my beauty.

"Of the men who went with me from Stanton-Corbet, two or three are hurt slightly, but none are killed save poor Jack Martin, who was shot down close at my elbow, while behaving with great bravery. Tell his mother from me that her son was a good soldier and a good man, and I make no doubt is now in a better place. And do you, my love, see that both she and poor Anne have proper mourning at my expense. The good widow must henceforth have her cottage rent-free and a pension.

"I will write more particularly in a day or two. Such another Sunday I trust never to pass. It would break your heart to see the village of Blenheim, so neat and thriving a few days ago, now a smoking mass of ruins, strewed with dead and disfigured corpses, and the poor inhabitants scattered no one knows where, all their little property destroyed or ruined. I can write no more now, as I must sent off this within an hour. Let the messenger have good entertainment."

Tears of mingled thankfulness and grief streamed down Lucy's cheeks. "Oh, I am so glad dear papa is safe! But poor, poor widow Martin, and poor Anne! She was so certain that Jack would come safe out of the war because the gipsy said so."

"Yes, and at the very time she was saying the words, poor Jack was lying still and cold in his bloody grave," said Cousin Deborah. "You see this battle happened a week ago last Sunday. And your father, whom she threatened so, is safe and well, and the thimble is found. So much for the gipsy's predictions."

"But, cousin, it is very odd about the thimble!" said Lucy, diverted from her letter for a moment. "Where did you find it?"

"Standing on the table beside the box."

"I do not understand it," repeated Lucy. "It certainly was lying there under the aloe-leaves when I went out with you that day."

"Perhaps Robbins picked it up and laid it upon the table," said Cousin Deborah. "He might have done so, and then forgotten all about it, for he grows more and more forgetful all the time. But now, my love, go and write the good news to Aunt Bernard, while I look after poor Anne."

Lucy's own part of the letter was as follows:—

"DEAR AUNT BERNARD:—This came in a letter from my father last Tuesday, and Cousin Deborah bade me write it out for you. We have got news this day that there has been a great battle, and the English have beat, and my papa is well, only he has got a cut on his face, but poor Jack Martin, Anne's bachelor, is killed. Dear Aunt Bernard, I know I was a naughty girl a great many times, and I hope you will forgive me, as I do you. I hope you will excuse blots, for I cannot help crying when I think about poor Jack Martin and his mother."

"That will do very well!" said Cousin Deborah, when Lucy showed her the letter. "No, you need not copy it. Send it as it is."

So Lucy sent her little letter to Aunt Bernard; but I am sorry to say she never received any answer.

When any one has gone on for many years like this poor, unhappy lady, indulging the passions of anger, pride, and an unforgiving temper, the heart sometimes becomes so hardened that it seems impossible to make any impression upon it. Possibly Mrs. Bernard may have been sorry in her own heart that she had been so cruel to Lucy, but she never said so.

When Anne had a little recovered from her grief at the loss of her sweetheart, Cousin Deborah talked with her seriously about the fault she had committed in helping Lucy to deceive, and in going with her to meet the gipsy-woman. Anne acknowledged her error and promised to do better. And Cousin Deborah took care to avoid all risk, by keeping Lucy with herself till the child had framed the habit of being truthful and open. This was not gained in a day, for bad habits are hard to overcome.

But Lucy was very much in earnest, and under Cousin Deborah's gentle and wise government, she had few temptations to hide her faults and mishaps. By degrees, she lost the frightened, crushed manner which had grown upon her under Aunt Bernard's reign. She grew strong and active in mind and body, and at the end of a year could work in the garden, walk, ride, and run races as well as Polly Burgess herself.

Hannah, who now and then saw her playing with the little girls at the rectory, or going about to see the poor people, reported to her mistress that the child had grown a regular tomboy.

And when Lord Stanton came home at the end of a year, he professed himself perfectly satisfied with the manners and appearance of his daughter, and begged Cousin Deborah to take up her permanent residence at the Court, and continue to superintend Lucy's education. Mrs. Corbet made her arrangements accordingly, and she remained with Lady Lucy till long after she was a married lady, with little ones of her own about her.

Lucy never heard any news of her knife. The gipsies decamped on the very day that the news came of the battle of Blenheim, nor did the same tribe ever visit Stanton-Corbet again.

It turned out as Cousin Deborah had supposed, that old Robbins had picked up the thimble and laid it on the table where Cousin Deborah found it, and, as usual, had forgotten all about it the next minute. Lucy used it every day, and never again forgot to put it in its place.

When Mrs. Bernard died, some years after, Lady Lucy gave old Margery a pretty little cottage and garden, and to wait upon her, a little orphan girl, the child of a fisherman from the cove below. This was the first revival of the Stanton-Corbet almshouses, which had been founded by another little girl, in the days of Queen Elizabeth, and of which we may perhaps hear more some day.

Another cottage was inhabited by the Widow Martin, and a third by an old soldier, who had accompanied Lucy's father all through the war, and came home with only one leg, to die in his native village. Lucy found great pleasure in visiting and working for these poor women, and her sewing hours no longer seemed the most tiresome part of the day, when she was making an apron for one, or a Sunday cap and apron for another of her old friends.

**THE END.**